PETALS OF THE CHRISTMAS ROSE

A CLAY AND DEEKIE
1875 CARTERSVILLE NOVELLA
BY DAVID AND MARIE TRAWINSKI

"Petals of the Christmas Rose" by David and Marie Trawinski

Copyright © 2025 David and Elizabeth Marie Trawinski, All Rights Reserved

v1.1

This is a work of fiction. The events and characters described herein are imaginary and are not intended to refer to specific places or living persons. The opinions expressed in this manuscript are solely the opinions of the author and do not represent the opinions or thoughts of the publisher. The author has represented and warranted full ownership and/or legal right to publish all the materials in this book.

This book may not be reproduced, transmitted, or stored in whole or in part by any means, including graphic, electronic, or mechanical without the express written consent of the publisher except in the case of brief quotations embodied in critical articles and reviews.

Edited by Elizabeth Marie Trawinski.

Published by DAMTE Associates Publishing LLC.

Cover Design Layout Copyright 2025 by David Trawinski
        using Adobe Stock Licensed Image
        as listed in Appendix B: "List of Cover and Interior Images."

Interior Images © 2025 David and Elizabeth Marie Trawinski unless otherwise
        attributed in Appendix B: "List of Cover and Interior Images."

Dedicated to

The Memory of

A True Father of Cartersville,

Colonel Lewis Tumlin

(1809 - 1875)

Christmas, 1875
Cartersville, Georgia

This novella is set in Cartersville in December of 1875. This was a difficult time as the entire country was going through what we now call "the Long Depression," started two years earlier by the Economic Panic of 1873. This instability would persist until the end of the century. It was known at the time as "The Great Depression" until this awful title would be usurped by the poverty and misery of the 1930s.

We have relied heavily on the archives of the Bartow County History Museum for the details used throughout this work, hoping to keep it as true to those times as possible.

We also have heavily accessed the digital renderings of the Cartersville Express Newspaper throughout this novella. Our great appreciation goes out to the Digital Library of Georgia, along with the University of Georgia, and the Galileo group for making these local newspapers available online. A great thank you is also extended for their being made available through the generous funding of the R.J. Taylor Jr. Foundation.

The Colonel and the Gypsy Woman

We wished to pay homage to one of Cartersville's founding fathers, Colonel Lewis Tumlin, who passed away in the year of this tale, 1875. All descriptions are taken from historical records and are footnoted throughout this work. In no way have we intended to fictionalize the life of this great man whatsoever, except in his bestowing his typical generosity to the fictional characters of this novella. We only wish to remind today's citizens of the love that this city long held for the Colonel, due to his staunch support for the town of Cartersville and the county of Bartow, formerly Cass.

On the other hand, the character of the gypsy woman and other gypsy characters in this work are purely fictional. We use the term "gypsy" as it was common for the time, and we wished to use it to stay true to the vernacular of that period. We mean no ill intent by its usage.

In reality, these wandering people were the Romani, a proud Indo-Aryan nomadic band not to be confused with the Romanian or Roman peoples. The Romani came early to the Americas, reportedly as slaves on Columbus' third voyage of 1498. They were known specifically to be in all regions of the state of Georgia, as well as throughout most of the United States by the end of 1875.

"To Love Another Person

Is to See the Face of God"

Victor Hugo

(1802 - 1885)

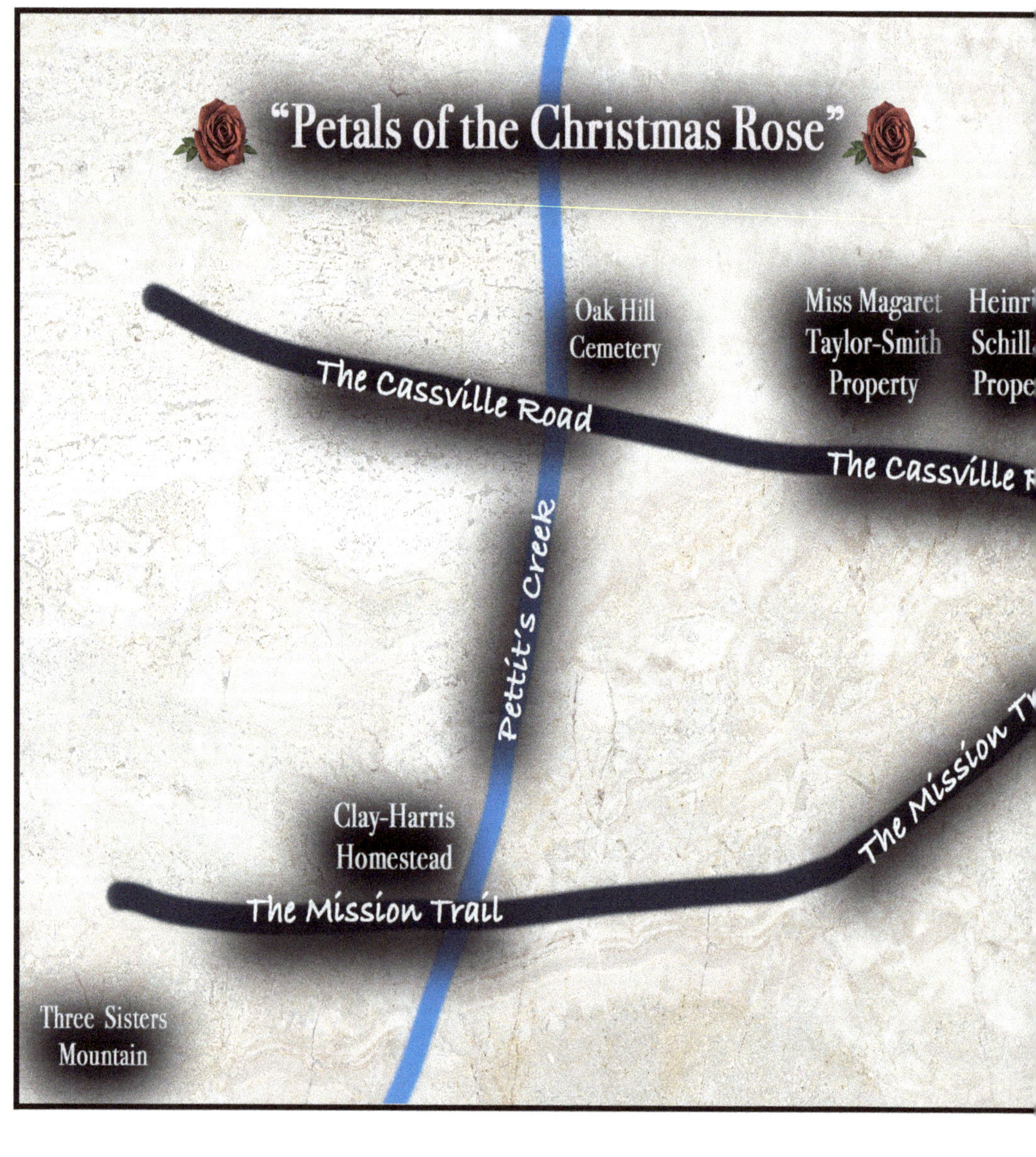

"Petals of the Christmas Rose"
Oak Hill Cemetery
Miss Magaret Taylor-Smith Property
Heinri Schill Prope
The Cassville Road
The Cassville R
Pettit's Creek
The Mission Tr
Clay-Harris Homestead
The Mission Trail
Three Sisters Mountain

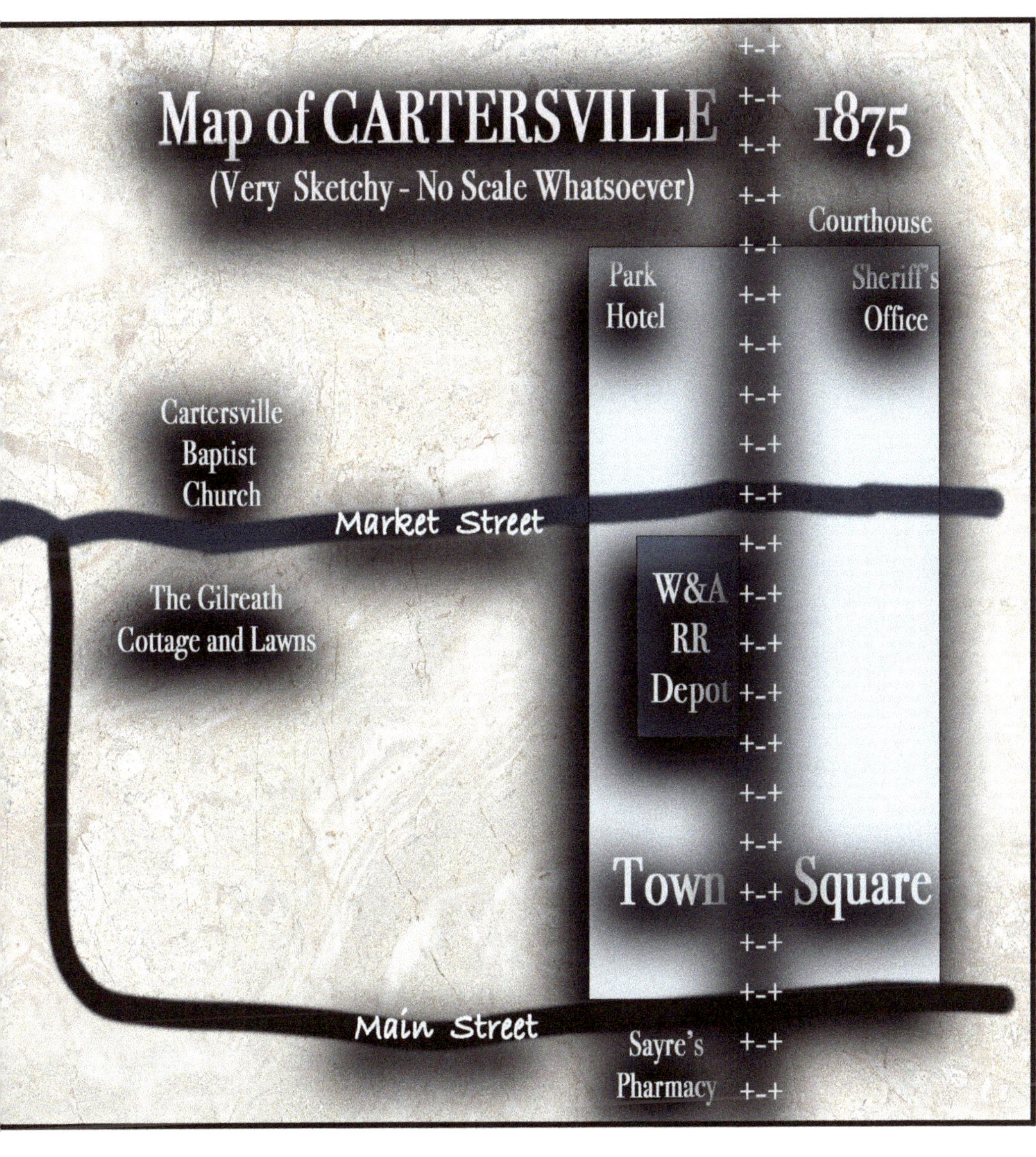

Map of CARTERSVILLE 1875
(Very Sketchy - No Scale Whatsoever)
Courthouse
Park Hotel
Sheriff's Office
Cartersville Baptist Church
Market Street
The Gilreath Cottage and Lawns
W&A RR Depot
Town Square
Main Street
Sayre's Pharmacy

Chapter One

Visit to A Downed Hero

He stood in darkness. A vacant loss pervaded the soul of Virgil Clay-Harris. It was made ever more hollow as the sharp sting of a thickening dusk chased away the last remnants of the first day of December, 1875. Clay stood staring, squinting all the harder as the darkness descended, at the marker in front of the crypt recently erected in Oak Hill cemetery. This final resting place contained the remains of the man who had not only lived most his life in Cartersville, but one who was largely responsible for the town being made into the county seat it had become. Here lied the remains of not only Clay's own personal hero, but the man who had meant so much to so many others in the county and beyond. Here rested the remains of the highly respected father of Cartersville, Colonel Lewis Tumlin.

Clay wondered just how much the Colonel's soul had been allowed to rest as his grave had drawn large crowds for months after his death in early June. So many wished only to lay down their flowers and pay their respects. Clay had walked over many times to do the same, only to find others keeping vigil before the crypt. He would turn away, knowing he must wait to come back alone. Only then, out of the sight of all others, could he give into the emotions that he knew would stir within him.

As the December chill settled heavily into the air around him, Clay faced the eternal truth of the crypt's exterior - all men, himself included, would one day come face to face with their maker. That cold, hard fact contrasted vividly to the warm and soft memories of the man whose body lay within. Clay fought back his emotions as he realized the flesh and bones before him were as lifeless as the decorative stones that encrypted them.

Clay shuddered. *It was the night air,* he thought. He pulled his woolen jacket tighter over the stump of his lower left arm, but despite this, his body quaked again. Only then was he aware of a lone tear tracking down his cheek.

Colonel, ya' were a good man, he thought. *No, ya' were the best of any man I had ever come to know, in fact. Ya' helped a poor old battered soul like me, long after so many others had no use for a one armed fella' than to be the root of so many stories of the War of the Rebellion. The Sharpshooter of Sharpsburg, such was the nonsense they spewed after the war. They made me a hero all over again after the shootout on Three Sisters Mountain.[1] Next they exaggerated how I took out that robber feller with a mile long shot from that Whitworth rifle in Texas. While they did li'l else but yak away, ya' gave me work, made me useful.*

Truth was, I missed that shot from up on Three Sisters Mountain to take out my childhood friend Willet, leavin' Deekie to settle that score. And that fat feller in Texas, well, I hit him alright, but only enough to knock him down and have need for that Cord McCullough trailhand to finish the job. But these townfolks don't let the truth stand in the way of a good story. They got nuthin' better to do than revel in them tall tales they created 'bout me.

---

[1] Former name of Ladd's Mountain per "The Light of Other Days" by Caroline Couper Lovell.

Stories, I reckon, are their form of forgettin' how hard their lives are, even if they get the facts all wrong. Colonel, yers are the stories they should be tellin'. Y'are the town's true hero. Colonel Lewis Tumlin is gone forever, but the memories of his kindness and generosity should live on forever, he thought.

Clay recalled how startled he was when Deekie read to him from the town's *Standard and Express Newspaper* back in June. The words haunted him even to this day, some six months later. Clay remembered them all nearly by heart, as the sound of Deekie's voice read them in his mind.

DEATH OF COL. LEWIS TUMLIN

This community was violently shocked, yesterday morning, to hear that Colonel Tumlin had departed this life during the night. He had been ill for several months, and was generally thought to be approaching his end, yet the announcement of his death was received with considerable surprise. He was about 66 years of age. Colonel Tumlin was greatly esteemed in this county by all who were familiar with the goodness of his heart and the general excellence of his character. He was one of the truest and most charitable of friends, and was bountifully generous and kind to those who won and deserved his respect. He was an affectionate and indulgent husband, and among the best of fathers. His very name is synonymous with industry and enterprise, and he had acquired one of the finest estates in North Georgia. [2]

---

[2] Cartersville Standard and Express Newspaper, June 3, 1875.

In every respect, Colonel Tumlin was one of our best and most respected citizens, and we mourn with his family for their great loss. His funeral will take place at the Baptist Church in Cartersville, tomorrow morning at 10 o'clock, whence his remains will be carried to the Tumlin Family Burying Ground, and there interred. It is suggested and earnestly hoped that every business house in the city will close doors, at least while the obsequies are transpiring. It is a manifestation of respect and esteem not undeserved by Colonel Tumlin. [3]

Indeed the town had shut down that sad summer day. Afterwards, drove after drove of well-wishers wore out a path to his grave, but now that the air was cooler and town readied itself for Christmas, that stream died down to a trickle. So, late this day Clay figured to be as good a time as any to pay his respects. He would not allow Deekie to join him, not wanting even her to see him become moved. Yet, as he stood here, he was on the verge of exactly that, of his watering eyes releasing a deluge, but he stayed strong and shed only one lone cold tear.

Clay was not generally an emotional fellow. Living through war as he did will wring so much of that out of a soldier, leaving him cold and brittle. Still. the Colonel had always been so warm and kind to him. While others could only tell the fictionalized exploits of this mangled wreck of a man, Colonel Tumlin had put in a good word for him with Nelson Gilreath, who gave him a job as groundskeeper after the war. That was then when things were bleakest for Clay and his family, and tending the Gilreath cottage lawn and its roses on Market Street saved them all back then.

---

[3] Cartersville Standard and Express Newspaper, June 3, 1875.

The Colonel had done more for Clay than merely to pass on good words on his behalf. When Clay came back from Texas after an impulsive adventure seeking out his long lost *"Diddy,"* it was amidst the deep pain of the Great Depression[4] when the bite of poverty was deepest. Colonel Tumlin gave Clay a job tending his own family's grounds. He knew Clay had been denied work due only to having lost half his left arm below the elbow at Chickamauga. Yet, where others saw a only a cripple, the Colonel saw a man who needed a job, not to heal his mangled flesh, but to salve the loss of pride and self-worth suffered in his soul.

Clay's stump below his left elbow began to itch in a most aggressive way. Clay scratched at it up through the empty jacket sleeve, but only after checking to see if anyone had drawn near enough to see, which they had not.

I guess that itch is yer thankin' me in the only way ya' can, Colonel, for comin' out to pay my 'spects. Truth be told, I am here to thank ya' for always treatin' me like a man, not a myth nor a cripple like this town's folk did. Then ya' hired that fancy lawyer to lay claim to that Texas reward money for me and Deeks. Them Texans reckoned they could get off Scott-free as we was from out of state, but yer lawyer fella' convinced them they owed Deeks and me that bounty. Damn if they didn't eventually pay up. Now that reward money was enough to keep me, Deeks and my brother afloat. Well, that and Truitt's salary as the Clerk of the Court. I should thank ya' for that as well, supportin' him the way ya' done durin' all them local elections.

---

4 "The Great Depression" was the severe period following the Economic Panic of 1873. It lead to the Long Depression which lasted until the turn of the century. The name "Great Depression" was later claimed by the financial collapse in the 1930s, which truly taught the nation just how "great" or severe a depression could be.

Ya' surely was a good man, Colonel, maybe the best I ever done knowed, or am likely to ever again come across. May the Lord Alrighty draw ya' tight to His bosom.

Then a dark thought crept into Clay's mind. *As ya' can be so convincin' in talkin' up a fella, can ya' put in a few kind words for me with the Almighty. He knows just how bad I am in need of His mercy fer sure, so a few kind mentions from a saintly feller like yerself can in no way hurt. Sure, I have killed enough men in my day, but I regret each and every life I took in the war. I also sincerely regret massacrin' all of Willet's bandits in their camp up on Three Sisters, as well as all the men that I was forced to lay harm to down in Texas. All I want is a peaceful life, and I hope in someway I can repay the kindness that ya' have shown me.*

Clay wiped the lone tear cooling heavily upon the skin of his cheek. He was ready to leave the Colonel to his perpetual rest, but before he walked off he wanted to read the inscription on the base of the fancy stone that served as his marker. He reached into his jacket pocket and took out the box of sulphur tipped matches he always carried. He extracted one and dragged it across the stone, until the friction rendered a flower of flame whose blossoming light he trailed in his sole cupped hand across its markings:

Col. LEWIS TUMLIN
Born May 19th, 1809
Died June 2nd, 1875
He rests from his labours

That much Clay could make out given the limits of his learning. *He rests from his labours,* he thought on the phrase. *Jus' how much rest is there for a departed soul as he awaits in the afterlife for his final judgement?*

Clay knew all about being judged. He had been judged all his life. A hero, a killer, a cripple, a sniper, a simple man, a semi-illiterate. He had always had to rely on Deekie for understanding any words more than a few letters in length. After all, she was the one doing all the reading, at least whenever she could steal away a few minutes. She had read the covers off the book with all the stories of Edgar Allen Poe in it. And that book he bought her in that fancy Peabody Hotel in Memphis, *"The Whale or Moby Dick"* by Herman Melville, she had consumed several times also. Now it seemed Deekie was always on Clay to buy her another novel, something that could take her away from the monotony of the household she ran while Clay and Truitt went off to their jobs. Clay thought there was not near enough money for the luxury of books, but Deekie promised she could read to him by the fire each night, just as she once had done with the Poe stories. He liked the idea of that.

"Come on, Virgil," she had once said to him, "I'll read a li'l of *Moby Dick* to ya' each night. Yer'll like it, too, and might even learn a li'l along the way."

"I don't reckon I am ever in this life gonna need to know anythin' about huntin' whales," he said, as she had told him that was what the story was about. "I don't figure to find any in the Pettit's Creek, now do I?"

"Virgil," she would say, "Yer mind is stuck in only what it knows, like a deep well it can't claw its way outta'. Sometimes it's good to learn how other people live. Like them whalers up in New England. This book tells of how they lived and hunted them whales in the seas all over the world. Ya' never know where life might take ya', do ya'? Did y'ever reckon on goin' to Texas in all the time 'fore we went and done so?"

"I have to say that I had thought on it," he admitted.

"Only cause yer *Diddy* done run off to Fort Worth with that woman. Before that ya' couldn't even find that town on a map. So, who knows when ya' might find yerself up in New England in one of them whalin' seaports."

"I done seen enough Yankees to fill all my days, Deeks," he would answer. "Now, that Poe fella ya' love to read so was from Richmond originally, makin' him a proper Southerner, so I don't mind so much hearin' what stories he had to tell. But these Yankee writers, I don't need them rattlin' 'round in my brain with their fancy tales glorifyin' their way of life. Not after the way they treated us after the war with their Radical Republicans freein' up them carpetbaggers to come down clamorin' all over us. So, I figure to pass on yer offer of readin' me *Moby Dick.*"

"That's yer dang problem, Virgil," he could hear the echo of Deekie ring out in his memory, "yer too simple a soul to ever make somethin' fresh and new of yerself."

The way Clay thought on things, he had let others complicate his life far too much already. The town's people had convinced him he needed to fight for the Confederacy, to become a soldier first, then a sniper, then the killer of men he never before knew. When he returned home they hung the titles of hero and cripple on him, one no heavier than the other, both millstones around the neck of a drowning man. Now, they judged him and Deekie as living in sin, the disgrace of the community.

As the match burned down, it licked his fingers with a slight searing. Clay brought his mind back to the present amongst the cemetery grounds around him. He looked back down at the marker. The birth date chiseled in it brought a smile to his face.

Even them fancy big city newspapers get things wrong time an' again. Clay was thinking on the words of the clipping from the Atlanta Constitution newspaper that Deekie had also read over and over to him:

Death of Col. Lewis Tumlin.

"Col. Lewis Tumlin died at five minutes past three o'clock this morning." This was the substance of a private telegram received here yesterday morning. Brief as it was, it contained much of sadness to many a household. Col. Tumlin was one of the most prominent men of North Georgia, and had long been long identified with it. He lived to see the wilderness blossom as the rose.

Col. Tumlin was born in Gwinnett county about the year 1811 or 1812. He went, when quite a youth, to Cass county as a volunteer to carry off the Indians. While engaged in this service he ploughed, barefooted, a crop of corn, and made that the nucleus of a large fortune. He settled there and amassed a princely estate. Full of energy, vim, persistence and hospitality he prospered in store and drew around him hosts of friends. He represented his county in both branches of the General Assembly several times and filled the office of Sheriff, all faithfully and acceptably. [5]

So, 1811 or 1812 per the Constitution clippin' actually turned out to be 1809, so says the marker, Clay thought. *I reckon' the stone to be right, as it was made by the man's family, and calls his birth to the day, May 19th. I always figured anythin' in the newspaper mus' had be true.*

---

[5] Atlanta Constitution Newspaper, June 3, 1875.

So, Colonel, ya' come out to Cass County to help carry off them Cherokee as a young man. That was also what brought my Diddy out this way, so he could put his claim in for some of that land down along Pettit's Creek. It's the land that me and Deekie along with my brother Truitt still live on to this day.

Clay put his tattered hat back on his head and began to walk away, when he thought a bit more on his *Diddy's* coming out to Cass County on the hope of winning some of the Indian land in the lottery. Word was that *Diddy* had gathered every red cent he could lay claim to and put up a bribe for the government officer overseeing that lottery. He had never heard *Diddy* talk of it, and had no evidence of the story to be true, but Clay figured it likely was. It sure sounded like something his *Diddy* would do.

These thoughts made Clay remember one last thing he needed to add to his discussion with the Colonel. He thought about pressing on home without returning to the crypt, but a feeling of dread swelled up in him as he did so.

So he stepped back and took his hat once more in hand. *Colonel, one more thing, when ya' sees my Maw, tell her I did go after Diddy down there in Texas. I done told her so, over her grave on our land, but she sure don't bother to give me no sign of havin' heard me. Not like ya' done by layin' that fierce itch on my stump. Tell her I done him right and freed him from them gang of sluggards that had imprisoned him for his gunsmithin' skills. Ask Maw to forgive him, jus' as Deeks and I have done for runnin' off with what cash we had on our way back to Cartersville. Well, maybe Deeks not so much as me, but he's still forgiven all the same. Diddy's not a bad man, the thing jus' is he gets caught all up in his greed.*

I keep prayin' for the man, that someday he'll do what's right and come back to us here in town, but my Diddy likely figures he's got a lot of carousing to do to make up fer all them years of bein' chained up by that gang. Still, my hope springs eternal. I promise in return fer yer passin' on this message to my Maw, I will do some further good on yer behalf in this world.

Strangely, at that moment Clay's stump of a left arm started itching again. A smile drew tight at his lips. *OK, then, a deal it is, Colonel. A deal it is.*

Clay stepped away for good. The night by then being fully dark, he decided instead of following the short path home along the banks of Pettit's Creek, as he would do in daylight, he would travel down the Cassville Road to where it joined Market Street[6] at the Gilreath Cottage lawn.

After all, coyotes had been known to attack stray dogs in those woods along the creek. Even though Clay still carried one of the guns his father had smithed for him, he thought it wise to not come across a pack of hungry coyotes in the dark. They likely wouldn't bother with a man his size, and would scatter after he shot the first one of them, but with it being mating season and all, Clay figured it wise not to even tempt the beasts.

Clay walked down along the Cassville Road instead. He thought it strange that it still bore the name of the town that the bastard Sherman had burned to the ground during the war. Clay figured it was the locals' desire not to let them Yankee sons-of-bitches have the final say by changing the name of the road. Of course, they were fine in ignoring the fact that the county name had already been changed from Cass to Bartow in '61.

---

[6] Then name of Cherokee Street, "Sketches of Bartow County," Compiled by J.B. Tate

The county had bore the name since its inception of General Lewis Cass, an old war hero and politician from Andrew Jackson's day. Yet as the War of the Rebellion drew near, only then did someone seem to notice that the man their county was named for was a Yankee.

That fact alone made Lewis Cass the enemy. He had even been nominated for President of the United States in '48 but lost to Zachary Taylor. Yet, when the war came in '61, the community's leaders despised the fact that the county was named after a man who turned out to be an abolitionist from Michigan. Even though the county changed its name to Bartow (after a proper Southerner in General Francis S. Bartow[7]), the county seat kept the name Cassville. After the war, it narrowly lost that prestigious posting to Cartersville, and the last hope of Cassville's revival thereafter died off.

Yet still, the name of the Cassville Road remained unchanged. The locals refused to rename it, that in doing so would somehow recognize Sherman's destruction of the former county seat. As such, Clay thought it to be as much of a road to nowhere as he could imagine.

At least Cartersville had the pluck to come back from Sherman tearin' up our town, he thought. *We're now the county seat, and got the courthouse down by the tracks - maybe a little too close to them tracks - and the town seems to be holdin' on through the Great Depression as well as any North Georgia town is. Things were tough, fer sure, but I reckon' that the town will find a way through it all. Cartersville had survived the war, after all, mangled and scarred up, jus' like me, but still here.*

---

[7] From the "History of Bartow County, Formerly Cass," by Lucy Cunyus, 1933.

Chapter Two

The German and the Gypsy

As Clay neared the end of the Cassville Road, he noticed a small crowd gathered at the corner near Market Street. For only being a dozen souls or so, they were creating one hell of a racket. Some one had lit up a torch and the crowd was huddled under its coarse flicker of flame around an older man holding on like grim death to the arm of a young woman who appeared to be in great distress. Most of the commotion was coming from that one man, and as Clay neared he recognized the rabble rouser.

It was that loud German immigrant who had come to town over the last couple of years. His name was Heinrich Schilling. The man had been all over Cartersville and the surrounding towns selling his decorative glasswares, most often a bit too forcibly for most of the local merchants. As much as Clay never liked the German's antics, he had never seen him as wild as this night.

"I tell you all," Schilling was screaming out in his heavily accented voice at the crowd, "Miss Margaret is deader than *der* last nail in a coffin, *und* it is *dis voman* that did it. She *muhst* pay for *killink* old Margaret Taylor-Smith, I tell you, *und* not through some court of law *dat vill* take forever *und* refuse to take her life, as *dey shoudt, yust* because she's a *voman* either, but…"

"What's all this ruckus about?" Clay yelled as he drew close and waded into the center of the agitated crowd. "Somebody needs to explain what all y'all are doin' out here and what yer makin' such a fuss over."

"*Dis gypsy Hexe kilt* my *neighbahr*, Miss Margaret Taylor-Smith," Schilling said, as he yanked hard at the young woman's arm, "by *schmuhshing* in her head. I *catch* her in the act. She *vas* stealing *deese* roses from Miss Margaret's hot house *vhen* the old *voman* confronted her. I *heared* Miss Margret scream *und* I *runt* into her yard, *und* I see *dis gypsy Hexe* standing over her with a bloody rock in her *hund* and blood all over her clothes."

"That's twice now ya' done said it," Clay interrupted. "What in blazes is a gypsy hex?" The fire from the torch flickered across the sea of angry faces in the growing crowd.

"*Hexe! Hexe!*" the German said excitedly, as if by repeating the foreign word it might somehow make it more clear. "In English, you *vould* say *vitch*. This *voman* is a *gypsy vitch.*"

Clay recognized the woman. She was the young gal who had been pedaling roses on the streets of town for the past few weeks. Word was she did so just to make enough money to survive. Some said she stole the flowers out of Miss Margaret's hot house, but others had said she took them with the elderly woman's permission. The latter was more likely, as Miss Margaret always was known to have such a soft spot for strays of all kind, after all.

"*Ve muhst* avenge Miss Margaret, here and now," Schilling said. His face was flushed red with anger, and the emotion wobbled erratically in his voice.

"T'ain't nobody gonna be doin' no 'vengin' this night," Clay said forcibly. "Miss Margaret's death is a matter fer the law. Now, someone run off and go git Sheriff Goff. The rest of y'all needs to be gittin' on home now."

"Vhat?" Schilling said with an incredible look on his face. "You say *dat yust* because your brother is Clerk of the Court. This gypsy *vitch vill* get off with the terrible lawyers you have in *dis* country. No, she *muhst* pay now! I *catched* her *red-hunded,* I tell you all!"

The crowd was growing larger and Schilling's words drove them into an excited state. Clay wanted only to calm things down before this all got too far out of hand.

"Whadya' have to say fer yerself, Ma'am?" Clay asked the young woman. The torchlight revealed not only that her face was painted in the direst of desperation, but that it was also smeared with ribbons of blood. She didn't offer up so much as a word in response.

The torch's flickering flame highlighted the violet hues in her long, tangled raven-black hair. She looked every bit of being guilty as the witch that Schilling had called her in his native tongue, but Clay was adamant that it would be the law that would judge her, not the taint of the torchlight nor the fury of the crowd huddled under it.

"I said whadya' have to say fer yerself, Ma'am?" The gypsy woman turned her gaze to him, but still did not speak. She was perhaps twenty-five or so, in the beauty of her youth and her scared eyes seemed to beg for mercy.

"Don't waste yer breath, Clay," a voice from the crowd said, "she don't speak no English. She's been stealin' Miss Margaret's flowers and sellin' them on the streets. Sheriff Goff already had complaints from Miss Margaret to that effect, or so says Herr Schilling, at least."

"I can't believe Miss Margaret is dead," A woman in the crowd began to wail. "How could this gypsy fiend do such a thing? That woman was over eighty years old. A murder in cold blood - I can't believe such evil could be happenin' here in our li'l town."

"Come *vith* me," Heinrich Schilling said, not to Clay, but to the crowd gathered tight around them both, as if the mob of townsfolk might be led to Miss Margaret's corpse and be urged into taking immediate retribution against the gypsy. "I *vill* take you all to *zee* Miss Margaret's *bohdy*. She is laying *dere* with her skull *smushed* in. *Dere* can be no question this *voman* did it. Look!"

Schilling thrust up the gypsy woman's left hand, which was drenched in a crimson slurry of blood. The sight of it, dripping down her arm, half caked at the edges, stirred the crowd into a frenzy. They could see her clothes were splattered with it. Miss Margaret had long been a favorite in town, for her heart was always full of such a special tenderness. She took in stray dogs like they were her own children. She was just as kind to any soul in need in town.

"Let's go see the body," one of the men in the crowd said. It had grown by then to a good two dozen townsfolk with more coming every minute, attracted like flies to the glare of the torch light and the din of the crowd.

"Yeah," another man agreed, "let's see jus' what this gypsy witch done to her."

"*I vill take you, but yust* the men *volk,*" yelled Schilling, "it is too *greezly* a sight for the *vomen* to *zee.*"

"Bring along the murderess, can't have her slipping off into the night." another man called out as the crowd started to follow Schilling to Miss Margaret's corpse.

"Dis goodt voman, Miss Margaret *vas* my neighbahr,"* Schilling said again, *"und* I insist that immediate *yustice muhst* be rendered …"

The blast of the gunshot split the night, immediately silencing everyone. After cowering in initial response to it, the crowd all looked up to see Clay's arm raised high in the night air, holding his smoking Colt Navy six-shooter.

"Like I was sayin', t'ain't nobody goin' nowhere," Clay yelled out. "Someone needs to go an' git the Sheriff. I don't care if Miss Margaret was yer neighbor or not, this is the law's business, not ours. So I'll take that gypsy woman and hold her until Sheriff Goff comes, Mr. Schilling."

"Herr Schilling," the German corrected him sternly, *"und* you are not *der* law here in *dis* town, Mr. Clay. I don't care if you have a *veapon* or not. No, I *vill* not turn this vile *voman* over to you."

"Then yer'll turn her over to me, *Herr* Schilling," Sheriff Goff said as he pressed his way through the crowd. "And Clay, what in the deuce have I told y'about shootin' off that pistol here in town. This whole crowd is near out of control already, all I need is for someone to be accidentally shot on top of all else. Now, what in the world is goin on?"

Heinrich Schilling excitedly ran through the events once more, but Clay detected his disappointment that the sheriff had arrived to take control of the scene. After listening intently, Sheriff Goff dispersed the crowd and instructed Herr Schilling to take him and Clay to view the body. A third man, Howard Gilmore, the sheriff's deputy, was taken along with the lantern he was carrying replacing the whipping frenzy of the torch's flame which slowly receded into the depths of the town's darkness.

Clay had holstered his gun to free his hand to take the arm of the gypsy woman from the German. As Schilling led them along, he limped noticeably.

"Ya' got a little hitch in yer stride, there, *Herr* Schilling?" Sheriff Goff, having noticed it also, called out.

"*Ya, ya,*" the German said, "*Die Hex* called one of the dogs on me. It bite me on my leg. She cast a gypsy spell on it. Look…" Schilling reached down to raise the cuff of his trousers. His ankle was torn up and bleeding hard.

"I *vill* be fine," the German said, "but be very careful *vith* this one." He pointed accusingly at the gypsy.

When they got to Miss Margaret's yard, sure enough, a dark lifeless mound, presumably that of her body lay just outside her backyard fence, on the side where her lot adjoined that of *Herr* Schilling's across a small creek. Only a few yards beyond it stood his large shed where the German made his glassworks. Between its slats of wood, thin shafts of lamplight escaped like fugitives in the night.

"Workin' late tonight, was ya', Herr Schilling?" Sheriff Goff asked.

"*Ya,* Sheriff, y*a,*" he answered. "I *vork* tonight. I *vork* every night. I make my *glassvares* to sell for *Die Weihnachtsgeschenke,* excuse me, that is Christmas gifts. *Den,* I hear Miss Margaret scream and I *runt* over here to find the gypsy *Hexe* striking her again and again *vith* a rock."

The German pointed to the darkened heap just outside Miss Margaret's fence.

"Bring that lantern over closer, Howard," Sheriff Goff said. "What is that layin' on top of her body?"

The lantern's light traced around the remains of an animal of some sort, lying as lifeless as the old woman herself. The gypsy girl spotted the dead animal and for the first time her facial expression of dire concern erupted into a sheer, unadulterated panic. She pulled away toward the woman's home from Clay's grip. Despite only having his right arm, the gypsy did not break free of Clay's firm grasp.

"It 'pears to be one of Miss Margaret's stray dogs she was always takin' in." Clay said as he fought to maintain his hold on the gypsy woman.

Sheriff Goff rolled his eyes. "That much I can see, Clay, but who would kill one of her dogs and lay it atop her so? That s'pose to be some kinda gypsy sign or such?"

Both men looked at Schilling, whose face was framed with as much a look of surprise as either of theirs.

"Do not look *dat vay* at me. *Ya, dat* is the dog that *bited* me. *Ya,* sure, I kick it *hardt* but I did not kill it. It yelped *und* run off. I did not even *zee dis* dog *vhen* I *runt after dat voman,"* he said. "Someone must have *kilt* the *hundt und* did *dis aftervard, vhilst* I chased the gypsy *Hexe* down *der* street until I *catch* her."

"So then, yer saying this young gypsy lady killed Miss Margaret with a stone and then run off," Sheriff Goff said, "and as ya' chased her down this dog bit ya', then ran off before ya' caught the woman and went into yer rabble rousin' down on the Cassville Road. All the while ya' did all this, someone took the trouble to kill Miss Margaret's stray and lay it atop her corpse?"

"Sounds like quite a tale to me," Clay said, and instantly drew a glare from the sheriff that said the question was not his to answer.

"Sheriff Goff," Schilling replied, "you *dun't* know *deese* gypsies in *dis* country like *ve* do in *der* Old Country. *Dey* are very dark people, practice black magic. *Verboten vitchcraft.* Maybe *der vitch* cast a spell on the animal. First to attack me, *und aftervard* to die for failing to halt me. Look, over here is *dat* rock *vich dis vitch* used to *schmahsh* Miss Margaret's head in."

Schilling reached down and picked up a bloody stone the size of a very large apple. It appeared to be quite smooth under its crimson-coated surface.

"Howard," he said to the deputy with the lantern, "hold that light closer to Miss Margaret's face so I can take a good look."

"Sheriff," Howard Gilmore said, "I'm gonna be sick if I do. I ain't never seen a murdered ol' lady 'fore."

"Okay, son," Goff said, "give it to me but stay close. I gonna need ya' still."

"Yessir, Sheriff," Gilmore said, all but thrusting the lantern at the lawman before backing off a few steps.

The sheriff swept over the corpse's face with its light. When he did so, he closely inspected the wound on the front of her skull. It was jagged around the edges, as if something sharp had caught and ripped open the skin of her forehead. The blood had stopped flowing and only traces of it coagulated thickly like dried syrup on the old lady's face.

"I'm surprised that such a smooth stone could tear away at the skin like that," Goff said to no one in particular. He motioned with his fingers at the edges of the wound, which were quite ragged, more like lacerations made by a knife's edge than the ripping of even the hardest strikes by such a small and smooth stone.

"*Vell,* Sheriff," Schilling answered, *"dis* one *muhst* have hit her *avfully* hard *vith* it, even many times before I got here. *Vhen* the rock hit her skull it might have *braken* loose some bone who's edges ripped away at the skin."

The sheriff's face appeared to suggest he was not buying that particular explanation.

"I'm also surprised there is not more blood here," the lawman answered. "Her face is near clean, save for this dried up bit by her eye."

"*Muhst* be *der* stray," the German said, "licked away *mohst* of it before it died on top of her. I tell you, *dere vas* blood all over her face *vhen* I left to grab this *vitch.* "

"Alright," Sheriff Goff said, "this is what we are gonna do. I am gonna stay here tonight with the body, so I can get a good look at the corpse come sun up."

"I *vill* stay *vith* you," Schilling said.

"No, Heinrich," Goff said, "ya' done had far too excitin' a night as it is. Clay will stay with me and keep hold of this gypsy gal. When the mornin' light comes up, after we get a good look at the body, we'll take her to a jail cell in my office and get the undertaker out here to retrieve the body. I assume yer okay with that, Clay?"

The look Goff cast at Clay suggested he had no choice in the matter.

"Sure, Sheriff," Clay answered, "but shouldn't yer deputy be the one to stay here with ya'?"

"He could, iffen he wouldn't toss up his guts by stayin' nearby," said the sheriff, "but I need to ask ya' a load o' questions about what happened tonight. We can go over all that while we wait out the break of dawn."

"Okay," Clay responded, "but Deekie and Truitt are gonna be a might worried if I don't come home a't'all."

"Damn," the sheriff said, "they will at that. Hey, Howard, can ya' walk down to Clay's spread. Stop in and tell Deekie what's goin' on? Then come back and I'll have ya' take this woman to the jail cell in our office."

"Sure, I'll go and tell Miss Deekie that Clay's here," the deputy said. "I need to do somethin' away from this corpse. I don't think there is any way I will sleep tonight after seein' Miss Margaret stone cold dead like she is."

"Then ya' best take the lantern with ya'," Clay said. "Deeks is got the matchin' pistol to this one I carry and if she hears somebody rootin' 'round in the dark, she's most likely gonna shoot first and ask who's out there afterwards."

The sheriff agreed and Howard Gilmore left with the lantern, leaving Clay, Goff and the gypsy girl in the darkness of the cold night.

Sheriff Goff called out to the German, who had begun to walk over toward his shed.

"Heinrich, how about the three of us stay in yer workshed until dawn?"

The German stopped in his tracks and walked back over to Goff. "You, Sheriff, can go in, but *nein* for *der vitch* or Mister Clay. I have *mein vorkshop* in *dere, und I don't vant* them seeing *vhat I do in dere.*"

"Okay, Heinrich," Goff said. "Best the three of us jus' wait out here in the open, then, but I may need to come by and see it later in the day tomorrow. I'd come now but I don't want to risk this gypsy gal breakin' free from Clay."

"Ya, ya," agreed Schilling before turning back to the shed on his property. The German walked over to the outside of his shed and then disappeared within it. A new glowing ball of light appeared as Schilling came back outside and took the lamp that had been hanging inside to lead his way up to his home. As he walked away in the distance, the young gypsy woman began shaking violently.

"Howard," Clay called out, "can ya' hold onto her for jus' a minute?" The deputy came over and took hold of the gypsy. Clay removed his jacket and held it out for the gypsy woman to take. She would not. Clay draped it over her shoulders, and thought only then her shaking was perhaps less to do with the chill of the night and more so with being so close to Miss Margaret's dead body.

Howard returned the prisoner's wrist to Clay's grasp. Then he left them to begin the walk down to alert Miss Deekie. As he walked away, the light of his lantern slowly shrank into the distance, bouncing along in the night's blackness erratically like a wounded, dying animal fighting off a predator's attack, until it was finally fully consumed by the ever-stalking darkness.

"Funny thing," Sheriff Goff then said to Clay as they sat in the blackness, their eyes not yet adjusted, "that German fella never offered us his lantern. Rather have us sit here in the dark. Maybe he doesn't want us to see whatever is lyin' next to us. Maybe he hopes we'll be too tired to notice all the details once the sun comes up."

"Yup," Clay replied, "might jus' could be."

Chapter Three

A Vigil Amongst the Dead

oward Gilmore went off to Clay's spread to tell Deekie what had occurred. Sheriff Goff talked in the dark as Clay held onto the still wailing gypsy woman with his lone hand, when the lawman asked for his permission to draw out the matches he knew Clay carried from his jacket pocket. After Clay agreed, Goff took the box out from the pocket of the jacket around the gypsy woman's shoulders and stepped away to strike one to closely inspect the dead dog straddled atop the corpse.

"Woulda' been a might easier with that German's lamp," Goff said, holding the match in one hand, his other running over the dead animal. "It's the damnest thing, Clay. Plenty dark out here, but it looks like this mutt ain't got a scratch on him. Plenty 'nough ticks, fat, full and hanging' on for dear life, but no wounds to speak of. Even its ribs feel to be intact after Schilling claimed to have kicked it, as he said. How ya' figure it died?"

"I dunno," Clay said, "strangled, maybe?"

"I don't reckon so," the sheriff said. "After the ribs, I felt for the bones in its neck, thinkin' the same thing, and they all seem to be intact. Had it been choked, they'd be all cracked up. Damn if this ain't most unusual."

"Unusual in what way, Alpheus?"

The sheriff did not take kindly to Clay using his Christian name in such a familiar way.

"Let's stick to 'Sheriff Goff,' mind ya' kindly, Clay." Goff's terse tone said it all - he expected Clay to keep their relationship in its proper order. Then he got back to what he had been saying before Clay's offense was committed. "I mean it's unusual in the sense that Miss Margaret come caterwaulin' to me a while back…"

Clay couldn't help from interrupting him, again.

"Yeah, I done heard 'bout that. Before ya' come along last night, Heinrich was tellin' the crowd that Miss Margaret was complainin' to ya' about this one," he yanked the gypsy girl's arm up slightly, "stealin' her hot house roses to sell on the street and all."

"Naw," Goff corrected him, "she never raised that at all with me. Fact was that I think Miss Margaret was lettin' the young woman take some of them to sell. Naw, Miss Margaret was all riled up that someone had killed off one of her other strays. I found the dog dead in her yard. She had accused Heinrich of poisonin' it. By the time I came out to take a look at it, the stray was bloated up like a blue ribbon hog at a county fair. I couldn't tell much, but I didn't find any wounds on it either. So I talked to Heinrich and he said he didn't know anythin' about it, but he was insistent that he did nothin' to harm the animal."

The sheriff kept periodically striking matches as the previous ones burned down to nothing more than a hot curl of ash. Under the weakly flickering light of each new match's flame, he examined the crime scene. As he did, Goff could see just enough around the woman's body to make out scattered petals of roses taken from her hot house.

"Come to think of it," Goff said upon seeing the petals, "Miss Margaret did mutter somethin' about her Christmas Roses dying off mysteriously, as if Schilling had somethin' to do with that too. When the sun comes up I'll sneak into the hot house she keeps, er…, kept in the yard and have a gander at them roses. Maybe she figured this gypsy here was doin' somethin' to kill them off in some way. Perhaps she confronted the woman and things came to blows, jus' like the German says. Miss Margaret always did get right peculiar about her flowers and shrubs, after all."

"Peculiar enough to die fer them?" Clay asked.

"Two things ya' learn in my line of work. People will fight over anything, and sometimes that leads to where ya' might never 'magine."

Having burned down the last of the wooden matches, the sheriff then looked up at the moon which had climbed high into the night sky. He appeared to be perplexed, and acted as if somehow staring at that heavenly orb might allow him to make sense of all the conflicting information. By then, all his clues were once more shrouded in the moon's dimly lit darkness all around them.

The sheriff sat down on the small hill alongside Miss Margaret's corpse. Clay followed him and dragged the gypsy woman with him until they stood over Goff, but on the side farthest away from the body. Clay sat himself down on the slight hill and then motioned for the crying gypsy woman to do the same, but she would not. Clay had to forcibly tug her down alongside himself. When he did, she began to shake, with Clay able to feel through her wrist the shuddering of her shoulders. He came to wonder if her reaction was from the terror of being so near the corpse, or from the crippling remorse of having killed Miss Margaret.

"Whatever happened here tonight," the sheriff said, as if reading Clay's thoughts, "I don't right think old Miss Taylor-Smith ever saw it coming."

Then, he heard Clay choke back half a chuckle.

"Whatever are ya' guffawin' at, Clay?" Goff asked. "I don't see much of anythin' funny goin' on here, I got a dead woman, a bloated dog and a wailin' gypsy to boot."

"I was jus' thinkin' on my *Diddy*," Clay responded. "When I was a boy, I asked him why we had that strange dash in the middle of our double last name. I always wondered 'cause no one else I knew had one in their name, nor did they have double last names at all, but I didn't know 'bout Miss Margaret then."

"And yer paw told ya' what 'zactly?"

"*Diddy* tol' me he figured it to be fancy to have a double last name with a dash. It was then he first tol' me about Miss Margaret, how her family name was Taylor-Smith. He thought that she was classy, and it didn't hurt that she had a lot of money. *Diddy* was always partial to people with money. Well, maybe he was jus' partial to the money. Anyhow, ma Maw years later said jus' 'fore I was born that *Diddy* changed our family name from Harris to Clay-Harris, to make it sound more 'spectful."

"Ya' know Miss Margaret is…, I mean was…, a Yankee, don't ya'?" the sheriff said, his tone half-accusing the dead women of having gotten outta life without doing time for that heinous crime committed at birth. As nice as a woman as she was, being born a Yankee was unforgivable.

"No, Sheriff, I did not know that. I took her to be as Southern as a cotton patch," Clay answered.

"Them dashed dubba-names is somewhat common in those Yankee high-falutin' types," Goff said. "Miss Margaret come down south from Connecticut years ago, about a decade before ya' was born, Clay."

"Really," Clay said. "What brought her all the way down here?"

"Her brother," Goff replied. "He had come down here to start up a mining business and was hurt in a bad accident while doin' so. Poor man never walked again after it, they say. She come down to take care of him and stayed until he passed on some ten years later. By then, she had learned to love it here. She had always professed to bein' somewhat of an *ama-tore* horticulturist and she jus' loved them flowers she could grow here, even in the dead of winter with that hot house she had put in."

By this time, the young gypsy girl had laid back in the grass against the small hill they were resting on. Clay still had a hold of her wrist. The girl still cried, but less frantically so, into the crook of the elbow of her other arm.

"What 'zactly is a *whore-tee-culchur-est?*" Clay asked, still not loosening his grip on the gypsy woman.

"Jus' a fancy name for a master gardener who grows many types of plants and flowers and such," Sheriff Goff explained. Then he added, "Ya' know, a lotta people thought it rather low of yer daddy to be dublin' up his name back then the way them Yankees did. Where did he even get the Clay part from?"

Clay knew his *Diddy* never did give a damn what the townsfolk thought of anything he did. The man was a free spirit, did what he pleased. Including abandoning us all, supposedly taking off for Texas with another woman.

"That 'Clay' part was a funny story," he chuckled lightly as he recalled the answer. "As Maw used to tell it, she was pregnant with me, and *Diddy* wanted to name me Clay. She was steadfast against it, and demanded for me to be named Virgil. So, he jus' tacked it instead onto his last name and that is how we become the Clay-Harris family."

"And everyone jus' went on to call ya' *'Clay'* all the same," Goff said, "jus' as yer daddy wanted."

"Made my Maw madder than a poked nest of hornets," he said, as the soft smirk lingered across his face. "She refused to call me by it. Never did once. Since she's been gone, only Deekie calls me by that proper name anymore. Even my brother Truitt long done give up in callin' me Virgil. It's *'Clay'* to him like everyone else."

It was then that both men heard the relaxed breathing of the gypsy woman. She had cried her self out and surrendered in to her exhaustion. Were it any louder, they would have called it snoring. She lay in the grass alongside Clay, who still noticing her shaking slightly, but this time from the cold, no doubt.

The night air had that kind of sting to it, he thought, and this girl was only dressed out in clothes as one might walk 'round the house in. No coat or other warm clothing, except for his jacket draped over her shoulders.

"Seems strange that if Miss Margaret did indeed catch this one raiding her hot house, that she was not wearin' a coat, a shawl or nuthin'" Clay said to the sheriff. "Looks like she was dressed for the indoors, don't it."

Goff looked over at the young woman. His eyes had adjusted by then to the moonlit night, and what he said next surprised Clay.

"So it does, Clay, Ya' know, she seems awfully relaxed fer a woman who supposedly jus' been caught after killin' another human bein'. Not jus' caught, but in the act with with blood on her hands and splattered all across her clothes and face. Hell, she's got more of Miss Margaret's blood on her face than the dead woman has on her own. Somethin' 'bout all this jus' don't seem to add up."

"Yeah," Clay said. "I noticed when Herr Schilling raised up her hand, it was her left hand that was drenched in blood."

"So, what 'bout it?" Sheriff Goff asked.

"Well," Clay went on, "every time she wiped her eyes from cryin', or to keep from lettin' tears loose, she's been usin' her right hand."

"Maybe she jus' doesn't want the old lady's blood in her eyes? Ever think of that?" Goff said.

"Might could be. Time will tell if she's a righty or not, but how ya' reckon to figure this all out when nobody here even speaks her language?" Clay asked.

"It's worse than that, son," Goff said, "as I don't even know what language these gypsy folk talk in. Who do I even call on to find out? I might have to go and send a telegram over to them folks at Franklin College[8] jus' to find that out. With a li'l luck, they might have someone over there in Athens that knows the answer, and if we're luckier still, might even speak it a lick or more of it, too."

---

[8] Franklin College was the original name for what became the University of Georgia.

Chapter Four

A Jaunt to the Jailhouse

Time passed and before too long the night sky slowly yielded to morning. As dawn just began to break, the glow of Deputy Howard Gilmore's lantern reappeared in the distance. Both Clay and Sheriff Goff watched as the sway of the lantern grew larger along with the three figures under the casting of its amber glow. Howard Gilmore led Deekie and Truitt to where they sat alongside the lifeless body of Miss Margaret.

"Virgil," Deekie yelled out as they approached, "what ya' dun got yerself into now? Couldn't jus' come straight on home, could ya'. Gotta go meddlin' in other folks' affairs. Howard here explained it all as we walked over."

Her voice roused the dozing gypsy woman, stirring her from her slight and surprising slumber. As she awoke in the lightest hues of dawn's advance, she spied the dead woman's corpse and began to shake in terror again.

"I didn't 'spect him to bring ya' over here, Deeks," Clay said, then looking at his brother, added, "ya' neither, Truitt. I jus' wanted ya' both to know I was alright but wasn't comin' home. Y'all got here fast 'nuff, though."

"We took the short way and come up the path alongside the creek," Truitt answered.

"Wasn't y'afeared of the coyotes?" Clay asked.

"Why should we be?" Deekie answered. "Howard had his light and I got this."

Deekie held up the old Colt Navy six that was the other half of the matched pair Clay's *Diddy* had converted over for him during the war. She carried it everywhere.

"Deekie," Sheriff Goff said, "didn't I tell ya' many times I prefer yer not to be wearin' that sidearm around in *my* town."

"Ya' done so," she answered, "and many times I have told ya', I am still gonna wear it all the same. Not like Virgil's got need for two handguns, is it? Not so long as he only got the one hand. I reckon I'll wear it, so long as it's legal for me to do so."

"Damn, ya' can be a hard case, woman," Goff said.

"She's right, Sheriff," Truitt added. "There is no ordinance in *your* town restrictin' her from wearin' it."

"Ya' know, Truitt," the sheriff said, "I wish ya'd stop fillin' her head with all those legal renderings. I know they're bound to be right, with yer bein' the Clerk of the Court and all, but doin' so only encourages her as to bein' looked down upon by the townsfolk."

"Sheriff Goff," Deekie said, "I don't give a good hoot about whether the town's ladies complain to ya' or not. They never had anythin' good to say about me no how, gun or no gun. They stick their sharp noses up in the air when I'm about jus' cause me and Virgil ain't properly married. Well they can all go to…"

"How about we calm down all this talk," Clay interrupted. "Ya' done rousted up the gypsy gal from her sleep, and I gotta hang onto her again so she don't run off."

The young woman already awakened by the sound of the voices she did not understand, responded to the sight of the dead Miss Margaret by moving in close to Clay. She reached out to lean into his intact right arm nearest to her. The resulting contact did not exactly escape Deekie's eye.

"Why she got yer coat draped over her, Virgil? She's awful pretty for bein' a witch," Deekie said sarcastically. Truer words had never been spoken, Clay thought. The gypsy had them long raven-black locks, full lips and high arching eyebrows. Under the flicker of the torch last night, her face looked taunt but smooth. The fear in her brown eyes made her look vulnerable.

Deekie did not care for how the gypsy clung to her man. She particularly objected to the way the woman pressed her full bosom up against him.

"Don't let her looks fool ya'," Howard Gilmore said, "she's a *muhrderess,* all the same. She needs to be kept from *killink* ever again." He mockingly imitated the acccent of the absent German, Herr Heinrich Schilling.

"Okay, let's forgo the foolishness and git back to business," Goff said, taking command once more. "Here's what we are goin' to do. First, Howard, use the keys to our office. Yer goin' to take the gypsy woman here and lock her up inside the middle cell. Ya' stay there with her until I come by later after full sun-up."

"Well," Deekie said, "I'm gonna go with him."

"Why on earth would ya' bother to?" Goff asked.

"Somethin' about this woman I jus' don't trust," Deekie said. "I want to make sure she makes it to jail, and doesn't somehow escape from yer deputy."

"I'll go with ya', Deekie," Truitt said, "and then we can walk back home together."

"I can't stop the both of y'all," the sheriff said, "jus' don't go shootin' no one while yer taggin' along, Deekie. All I want is to make sure is that woman gets locked up. As for you, Howard, that's yer responsibility to git it done. Don't leave her in that cell alone, keep watch over her until I come back in the morn."

"I tell ya', Sheriff," Gilmore said, "there ain't no way I can sleep after all this excitement. No, I'll stay in the office until ya' git back, don't worry."

"Fine. As the sun is now startin' to come up, I am likely not to have need of yer lantern soon. Go an' git this woman off to her jail cell."

With that, Howard took the arm of the gypsy woman. A fresh and greater fear ignited in her eyes, as she had come to trust Clay in their few hours together. Clay motioned for her to go with him. Yet before her Virgil could say anything to her - Deekie forgot for a moment that the woman would not understand - Deekie took her other arm.

"Let her go, Howard," Deekie said. "I've got her. She'll be less frightened that way."

As they began to walk away beside the fence along Miss Margaret's yard, the young gypsy pulled back defiantly and frantically toward the dead woman's house. Yet, Deekie would not allow the woman to keep them from departing off to the town square and Sheriff Goff's office.

"Here, Virgil," Deekie said, "take back yer coat. She's smeared blood all over it. Besides, it's downright col' out here in this mornin' air. Yer gonna need it."

"All the better reason to keep her covered with it," Clay said, despite knowing it would draw Deekie's ire. "Besides, the smeared blood will blend right in with all the dirt stains I already got all over it. Jus' take it home with y'after yer lock her up in the sheriff's cell."

Deekie gave her man a glance sharper than the winter air. Then, she turned her cold shoulder to him and turned to the two men, "C'mon, Truitt, Howard. Let's git on with it."

Deekie, Truitt and Howard took the lantern, and walked off in the direction of the town square. The streets were at that hour dead empty. The sky had changed from a moonlit black to that dark shade of cobalt that lingers just before the full majesty of dawn explodes into so many vibrant hues.

The gypsy woman fought them, constantly pulling back toward Miss Margaret's house, but Deekie resisted her. She nearly dragged her along as Howard and Truitt walked behind them to assure that the prisoner would not break free. All along the way this continued, with the gypsy woman pleading the same three words, *"Pliss, no, sorry…"*

Soon they crossed the town square, with the moonlight night slowly fading into the approach of dawn. The gypsy woman never gave up her effort to yank back, but the three of them pulled and prodded her forward. They made sure she moved toward Sheriff Goff's office.

When the three entered the office of the sheriff, Howard led the gypsy woman toward the cell. The woman became erratic again. The sight of the bars seemed to set her off. She grasped at the edge of the sheriff's desk as they passed it and said *"No, no, no. pliss, no. Sorry, sorry, no, pliss, sorry."*

Both Deekie and Truitt had been stunned to hear her speak any English at all along the way. They began to ask her simple questions, but to every one they asked all they got in return was *"Pliss, no, sorry!'*

Then Truitt said, "I think that's all she knows. Likely those are the only three words she uses to sell her flowers on the street."

Then, the gypsy spewed out something that neither of them could understand. It came in an unusual and most garbled tongue, tainted with desperation:

"Si man jekh tikno chavo. Voj trubul man."

"What the hell kind of language was that?" Truitt asked. "I never heard nothin' like it.

"I think she jus' cast a spell on us all," Howard said.

Then the gypsy woman released the desk, and with her two free arms formed an empty cradle and made a rocking motion. She turned her gaze toward Deekie, knowing she would understand. The sadness and anxiety in her eyes begged on her behalf.

"I think she's sayin' she's got a baby somewhere," Deekie guessed. "She needs to stay free to care for it."

The woman tilted her head at Deekie, in a way that any woman around the world would recognize. *Mercy,* the nod said, *please have mercy on me for my baby's sake.*

Then the gypsy woman said more in what sounded like the same garbled tongue:

"Me trubuj te dav xabe mure chavores."

As she uttered this, she grabbed at her breast.

"Oh, my Lord," Deekie said, "she's sayin' she has to go and feed her baby!" This realization shot a bolt of terror that ripped through her like a strike of lightning. Somewhere in the night out there was left a small, poor, defenseless child by itself, all alone, unprotected…

"Let's jus' get her in the cell," Howard said, "and Sheriff Goff will know what to do when he gets here after sun up. Jus' a couple hours more and he'll likely be here."

"Don't ya' see," Deekie said, "she's been out all night. If that child was left alone, God knows what could have happened to it overnight. It could've done froze to death. Suppose a pack of coyotes got at it? We have to let her take us to get that youngin, right now!"

"She could be makin' all this up, Deekie," Truitt argued. "Suppose she walks us right into a camp of gypsies. Then someone will have to come lookin' for us."

"Pliss," the woman kept saying, making a gesture holding here two hands close but apart.

"She's saying her child is very small, a baby," Deekie said, tears clouding her eyes. "It must be closeby, Howard. Let her take us to it. I got my six-shooter, we'll be fine. Come on, it can't be far off, won't take us very long. We'll be back and have her in the cell before Sheriff Goff even gets here. I promise."

"Damn it, Deekie," Howard said. "I'm gonna regret goin' along with this, I am sure of it."

"Don't be such a 'fraidy cat, Howard," Deekie said. "This is a real adventure. C'mon, let's go."

"She could be makin' this all up," Truitt echoed the deputy's earlier concern. "Deekie, ya' jus' love yerself a thrill every now and then. Somehow I think that gypsy woman senses that. I think she can see it in yer eyes…"

"I think Truitt's right," Howard agreed. "That gypsy done cast two spells on us and jus' wants to lead us off so her black magic can befall us and then she can slip away. She ain't got no baby."

"I beg to differ," Deekie said.

"How ya' reckon?" Howard asked.

"There's things about babies a woman jus' knows."

"What do ya' think you know about little ones, anyway, Deekie? Y'aint had none…"

"True 'nuff, but y'aint had none with Mrs. Gilmore neither, have ya', Howard?"

"Ya' know we ain't yet," he responded.

"Had ya' done so," Deekie said, "ya' might know what I already do. Ya' might have noticed them stains on that gypsy woman's blouse. Her milk's done come in. She's leakin' right through its fabric. She's got a little one somewhere closeby, fer sure needs be fed. Only question is where, and in what shape is it in after bein' left alone all night?"

Chapter Five

The Revelations of Dawn

The sky very undramatically lightened through ever-brightening hues as a very drab gray overcast sky had settled in, stealing away dawn's dramatic pallette. Still, layer after layer of truth was revealed to Sheriff Alpheus T. Goff and Virgil Clay-Harris. First off, the sheriff confirmed his overnight match-lit examination of the dead dog. It bore no signs of injury of any kind. In its deathly repose, it laid atop Miss Margaret's body as if guarding it. The heartbreak of finding its master lifeless had seemed to choke out the animal's last breath, and the stray joined in death she who had shown it such kindness in life.

The sheriff moved the carcass aside carefully, and laid it gently in the grass alongside the woman's corpse. As he did, Clay looked over the body of the dead dog.

"Sheriff Goff," Clay said to his companion's back, "did ya' happen to notice this animal's tongue."

"Yeah, Clay," the sheriff answered, "it hangs out an unnatural amount. That's what happens when they die, all the muscles relax and the tongue protrudes. God knows I seen enough dead varmints in my days to recognize that."

"Naw," Clay responded, "I seen dead dogs before 'nuff to understan' that. I mean on its tongue is all these little white flecks, as if it had been chewin' up raw rice."

"Let me see here," Sheriff Goff turned to face Clay and look over the animal once more. "Damn, if ya' don't have a sharpshooter's eye after all, Clay. What do ya' reckon they could be from?"

"No, idea a't'all," Clay answered, "but I figured I'd call yer 'tention to it. Could mean somethin' important later on. We might regret not havin' noticed it."

"Sure 'nuff," the sheriff said. "Damn I wish our town was big 'nuff to have a photographer here."

Clay smirked. "We'll this poor stray sure wouldn't have any trouble stayin' still for the time it takes to git its picture made. Not any more."

"Ya' got a blade wit' ya', Clay," Goff asked. "Try an' scrape a few of them flecks off its tongue if ya' can." Then the sheriff turned back to inspect the head wound that had laid Miss Margaret low. Laid her still, forever still.

Clay carefully wiped the flecks on to a clean spit rag he always carried but rarely used, as in his travels he tended to spit freely at most anything and everything that didn't move. As the daylight improved, he examined the deposits on the rag. The white flecks were hard to see on its cotton surface, so he folded the rag over and carefully placed it in his trouser pocket.

Sheriff Goff had turned back to examine the remains of Miss Margaret. "I'm still a might challenged to explain why this wound on Miss Margaret's head is so ripped and ragged. This gash don't look like anything that smooth rock would make, regardless of how bloody it is."

"Might could be that rock ain't what tore up her skull a't'all," said Clay.

"That's what I'm thinkin', but I don't see nothing' else about that could have ripped at the skin of her head so," Sheriff Goff replied.

"Sheriff," Clay said, "look at that track coming' down from the house outta Miss Margaret's yard. Looks like someone or somethin' was dragged out here."

"Could be from whoever dragged that dead dog out here," Goff surmised.

"Iffen ya' ask me, it looks too wide fer jus' that dog to have made, Sheriff."

Just then they heard a muffled cry from across the yard. "What in blazes was that?" Goff asked.

"Sounded like some 'coons fightin' over something," Clay said. "I heard it earlier in the night. Them things will do that, fight over scraps of trash and such."

"I don't know, Clay," Goff said, "that didn't quite sound like no racoons to me."

The wailing cry drifted out faintly again, but this time clearly from inside the house. Before Clay or the lawman could react, it was stomped out by the noise made by four approaching figures.

"Damn it, Howard," Sheriff Goff said, "I thought I told ya' to take this woman to the jail cell. What's she doin' back here?"

The soft wail repeated. The gypsy woman pulled frantically again toward the house.

"Ain't either of ya' got sense enough to go tend to that cryin' baby child?" Deekie said.

"What baby?" Clay asked.

"Virgil, honestly," she said, "sometimes I swear ya' didn't lose yer arm in the war but yer hearin'. There's a baby in that house cryin' out plain as day."

"That's what I was gittin' ready to tell ya', Sheriff Goff," his deputy, Howard Gilmore said. "This gypsy woman told us not to lock her up cause she had a baby needed tendin' to."

"So, all of a sudden one of y'all three speak fluent gypsy?" Goff chided. "Will miracles never cease?"

"Don't be such a horse's ass, Sheriff," Deekie scoffed back. "She done it through hand motions and such. But she did try an' make us know it by talkin' some gypsy gibberish that only the devil himself could understan'."

Then Deekie took the gypsy woman by the hand and led her over to the house. Clay's brother Truitt followed closely behind both women. Goff was still kneeling over the body of Miss Margaret, but he took a second to cast a glaring eye at Gilmore.

"Howard, ya' lose sight of that gypsy prisoner and there'll be hell to pay for both yerself and that Clerk of the Court. Now git in there after the three of them and make sure they don't disturb nothin' while tendin' to that baby, if there really is a chil' cryin' in there."

"I sure will, Sheriff," Gilmore said as he trotted off to catch up to the two women and Truitt. Goff and Clay stayed back with the corpse and the stray dog's carcass.

Deekie opened the back door to the house and the wailing became louder and more distraught. The gypsy woman pulled away from Deekie's grip and rushed toward the front parlor. Nestled in a blanket within a woven basket on the sofa was the infant. The gypsy lifted her baby, kissed it, and held it up tenderly to her shoulder. Then, with not a second thought, she unbuttoned her blouse and offered the child her breast.

"Oh my God," Deekie said, staring at the shelves of books along the interior wall of the room. "I ain't never seen so many books in one place before." She ran her fingers along the spines, reading the titles aloud: "Madame Bovary, A Tale of Two Cities, Crime and Punishment, The Count of Monte Cristo, the Less Miserables…,"

"No, Deekie, not less miserables," Truitt interrupted her, "it's pronounced *Lez Mees-er-robs.* "

"How the heck would y'even know that, Truitt?" Deekie asked, still scanning the array of book titles.

"Cause we jus' had a fancy *May-retta* lawyer pleadin' a case in front of Judge Ferris, and he referenced that book sayin' the punishment the prosecution was askin' for was akin to someone called John Val John gettin' twenty years for stealin' a loaf of bread in *Lez Mees-er-robs.* It's a French story and that's how they say it. At least that's how that fancy lawyer said it."

"Well, I ain't never heard of it and I don't speak no French," she bit back, "so it's the Less Miserables to me."

"Ya' country bumkin," Truitt snapped, "that's the opposite of what the book is even about. I asked that lawyer. It's not a tale of how less miserable these French folk lives were, but how hard they had it. It means "The Miserable Ones" Come on, say it - *Lez Mees-er-robs.*"

"I won't say it. It's silly soundin', and I won't lower myself in that way. Hey, there's a book missin' next to it." Deekie spun around, and scanned the room. It was then that Howard Gilmore entered. He immediately froze in place seeing the gypsy woman nursing her young one.

"What ya' so surprised at, Howard?" Deekie said to the deputy. "It's jus' a lady teat. Ain't no different than how yer chubby baby face was fed once."

"Not by a woman who might had jus' killed someone," Truitt defended Howard, still caught in surprise.

"Ya' got no room to talk, Truitt," she said. "Knowin' yer Maw as I did, I'm not sure she could pass that test. She was mean 'nuff to have killed any man in this here town."

Truitt cut her a mean stare. "Have some respect fer the dead, Deeks. That's my Maw yer talkin' ill 'bout."

"I tend to 'spect the livin' more than the dead," Deekie snapped, then turned. "Howard, stop starin' …"

"Sheriff told Howard to keep an eye on that gypsy," Truitt defended the deputy again. "That's all he's doin'…"

Deekie skipped past the space where the missing volume was to eye more of the titles shelved there. "Dang if she don't even got the same copy of *Moby Dick* that yer brother got fer me in Memphis. I don't see no Edgar Allen Poe here on her shelf, tho'."

Then Deekie spotted an open book lying on a small desk by the window next to a comfortable wing chair. She walked over and sat herself in its fine upholstery, and took the open volume into her hands. Her eye was drawn to a drawing of a gargoyle watching over the rooftops of Paris, reminding her of Poe's story, *Murders in the Rue Morgue.*

"Hey, here's the missin' book. By the same author as that Less Miserables story, Victor Hugo. Called *The Hunchback of Notre Dame.* Gots lots o' pretty drawings inside it. Looks like Miss Margaret was in the middle of enjoyin' it. I sure wouldn't mind readin' it."

"Don't ya' be thinkin' yer'll be takin' that with ya'," Howard said stiffly.

"Well, I don't reckon Miss Margaret is gonna be gettin' back to finishin' it anytime soon…" Deekie bristled.

"It's evidence," Howard reminded her. "This here is a crime scene. Put it back."

"This ain't no crime scene," Deekie argued. "Miss Margaret was killed outside and surely not by bein' hit over the head with some fancy book."

"It's still evidence," Howard repeated. "We don't know fer sure if Miss Margaret wasn't killed in this very room."

Deekie ignored the deputy and fanned through its pages. She found it to have many black and white lithographed illustrations included within its covers.

"Deekie, ya' put that book back, or I'll tell the sheriff and he'll make ya'."

"I don't figure yer likely to do that, Howard," Deekie offered up a threat of her own, "Or I'll tell Sheriff Goff how ya' knew all along it was Truitt who tossed that evidence knife used in that attack on the carpetbagger years back onto that passin' northbound train."

"Deekie!" Truitt said, alarmed that she would speak his secret out so openly.

"That's an outright lie," Howard Gilmore said, "besides, the whole town already done figured it was Truitt. It's old news. He was elected to be Clerk of the Court after all that. So even were it true, Sheriff Goff won't care one bit. Ya' got nothin' on me, so put the book back."

"I got plenny" Deekie said. "Y'ever heard of the seeds of suspicion? Once they get planted, it looks like nothin' is happenin'. Then, whether it takes a week or a month or a year, Sheriff Goff will start to wonder what else ya' been keepin' from him."

"But I ain't been keepin' nuthin' from him," the deputy protested. "I only suspected Truitt flung that knife, I didn't know fer sure."

"That's not what I'm gonna tell the sheriff," Deekie threatened. "Seeds, Howard, Seeds. Ya' willin' to risk yer job over keepin' this little ole book outta my hands?"

Howard Gilmore seethed. "It ain't right, yer threatenin' me with a lie and all."

To which Deekie cut him off, "It don't have to be right. It only has to sound right, Deputy Gilmore. Best I call ya' that while I still can. Who knows, maybe ya' tattle on me and we'll both end up in side-by-side jail cells. Now, I'm gonna hide this book outside so I can take it later, and yer not gonna say a word, are ya?"

"Oh, go ahead and borrow that damn book already," he replied, figuring it best to allow her to do so.

Deekie's stirring up the past caught Truitt off guard. He knew what he'd done back then was wrong, but reckoned it to be long forgotten. And here was Deekie confirming what everybody in town had already thought.

"It's a deal," Deekie agreed. "I won't say how ya' held back that it was Truitt who threw Willet's Black Raven dagger onto the car of that passin' train. We both stay mum on our li'l secrets and nobody has to know any better."

"I ain't never heard nobody but yerself call that dagger by that name," Truitt said, "surely Willet never did."

"Hush, boy," she said, "ya' never knew Willet Blackwell like I did. He always called that knife by that special name - the Black Raven."

"Ya' done read that straight out of yer collection of them Poe stories," Truitt said. "Don't y'even wanna fuss over the baby some. What kinda woman are ya', anyhow?"

"I done seen babies before," Deekie said. "I'll fuss over a child that's mine when that day comes along."

Despite her denying it, his comment stung. Deekie slowly turned her gaze onto the nursing gypsy mother. The child looked so content at her bosom. The sight seared a burning ache within her, as if the flickering tip of envy had scoured deep into the emptiness inside her. Deekie denied herself surrendering to this feeling of longing and moved briskly over to the door they had come in through.

With the deputy intentionally looking the other way, Deekie took the Hunchback book and slipped out the back exit of the house with it. She walked across the yard to the hothouse entrance. Once inside, she left the book behind a row of vibrant red roses. Then she walked outside, toward the gate in the fence. Inside its planking, she noticed were rows of shriveled up plants. She thought it funny because the creek ran just on the other side of the fence. Maybe they had taken up too much of its water? Maybe not enough? Either way, she noted them in her memory.

She then walked through the gate to where Sheriff Goff and Virgil were still examining Miss Margaret's body in the daylight.

"I thought ya' were inside with Howard, Truitt and the gypsy gal," the sheriff said.

"Don't worry none, Sheriff, Howard and Truitt's got their eyes on her, alright."

"And there really was a baby in there?" Goff asked.

"Yeah, sure was," Deekie answered, "and both boys got it and its mama in their sight, all the same."

"I figured she was tendin' to it," Clay observed, "as it stopped cryin' out so loud."

"My God, Virgil, yer surely sharp as a tack," Deekie said. "Ya' should become one of them Pinkerton Detectives. I guess they likely got an openin' after that one in Texas done got stabbed in the leg by that Cord McCullough fella. I figure that Pinkerton must be all played out by now."

"Why do y'always say his name like that, Deeks?" Clay asked. *"That Cord McCullough fella.* We both know ya' took a shinin' to that trailhand on that Texas trip. A little too much if ya' was to ask me."

"Will ya' both shut yer traps with all that jealous jabberin'," Sheriff Goff yelled out. "Deekie, we done been all over Miss Margaret's corpse here, ya' want to have a look with yer woman's eye in case we missed anything?"

"Can I, really?" she said. "Yer not joshin' with me?"

"No. Go ahead and tell me what ya' notice, no matter how small the detail may seem to be."

"Okay, let me have a gander at her," Deekie moved in real close to the corpse, but as she did she felt queasy. She figured it to be from being a little too close to the dead, but she would not let it keep her from her task. She tried to still herself so her squeamishness would not show through.

"Only thing I can offer up, Sheriff, is that the poor woman's face powder is all smudged up."

"Like she was puttin' it on in a hurry?" asked Goff.

"Naw," Deekie corrected him, "more like she was in the middle of takin' it off. Somethin' smeared it all up."

"Anythin' else?" Goff asked.

"Yeah, Sheriff," Deekie said, "Miss Margaret's head is bashed in and I think she might be dead."

"C'mon, Deeks," Clay snapped, "quit the tomfoolery and get serious."

"Damn wisecracker," Goff added. "Alright, I'll have the coroner come out with a wagon and take her body to the undertaker."

"How long ya' figure she's been dead?" Deekie asked.

"Not sure," Sheriff Goff admitted, "but likely sometime last night or so like the German said. Why?"

"Well, I noticed on the other side of that fence is a row of withered-up plants. Looks like maybe they was gettin' too much of that creek water or something. Seems odd a lady like Miss Margaret who was so fussy about her garden would ignore them so."

"Well, that does seem a bit peculiar. Are they in the hothouse?" Goff asked.

"Naw, they're outside in the open air on the other side of that fence," Deekie said, hoping to keep the lawman out of the hothouse and away from her freshly hidden Hunchback novel.

"Sheriff, what are ya' goin' do with that baby when ya' lock up that gypsy woman?"

"I didn't even begin to think on that, yet" the sheriff said. "If the woman is nursin' that chil', that's a problem. I can't have a wailin' infant in the jail cell with her."

"She is surely nursin' that baby," Deekie said. "There ain't no ifs 'bout it. Jus' ask yer deputy and Truitt, if ya' don't believe me."

"Maybe I could pay ya' to look after that chil' while that woman is in jail. Pay ya' two bits a day?"

"I got no way to feed that chil'," Deekie said. "It would starve to death. No thank ya', kindly."

"Naw, ya' could bring it by for the gypsy girl for a feedin' a few times each day," the sheriff offered.

"At that age, these babies eat at all different times. Besides, I'd have the better part of a mile's walk each way. Nope. Won't be happenin'."

Goff seemed annoyed at her resistance, knowing all along she was just dickering for more than two bits a day.

"C'mon Deekie," he said, "I can't have a cryin' baby in my office all that time until her trial comes up. I'll pay ya' half a dollar a day."

"One full dollar a day!"

"No, Deekie, best I can do is a half dollar a day."

"A dollar and ya' have that gypsy mama brought to my house so I don't have to carry that chil' out in the weather so much."

"A half dollar a day and I'll have Howard bring the baby to yer spread every other day to cut down on yer and the child's travels."

"Done deal!"

"Hold on, now, Deeks," Clay said. "We ain't even talked this over none."

"Hush, Virgil," she said. "Ain't nuthin' needin' to be jawed over. The baby needs a woman's touch, and I am offerin' my services to Sheriff Goff. If ya' don't like it, ya' can make yerself a bed out in the barn."

"We don't have a barn," Clay answered.

"I know." Deekie smiled, leaving him to figure out her gist as she returned to retrieve the hidden book in the hot house. She said out loud as she walked away, "I'll leave it to ya' menfolk to figure out how to tell that gypsy gal about our arrangement. I'll come down to yer office to gather the chil' up and take it home late this afternoon. That'll be after I make up for all the sleep y'all done stole from me overnight."

Chapter Six

Hidden Evidence

Later that morning, Clay sat at the oak table near the potbelly stove in his cabin. The warmth of the fire caused his face to sweat just a bit. He reached his right hand, that is, his only hand, into his trousers for his rolled-up spit rag. Truitt had already returned, changed his clothes and headed off to work at the court house. Deekie prepared to crawl back under the unmade covers scattered wildly on the tick mattress they shared.

"Dang it!" Clay swore out.

"What is it, Virgil?" she asked.

"I done forgot to give Sheriff Goff these white flecks I scraped off that dead dog's tongue."

Over the years, with Truitt and Clay working steady, they had managed to get a loan to finance the renovating of their one room shack, which was in dire need of a good shoring up. Afterwards, it was more a cabin than a shack. They added on an extra room as they rebuilt the former single room structure. The new bedroom was laid claim to by Truitt, as he argued that it was his efforts as Clerk of the Court that would be paying for most of it. Truth be told, it was Clay and Deekie's Texas reward money that paid down the bank loan years ahead of schedule.

Having that note paid off made life somewhat easier for the three of them, but even still, there was little money left to squander on much anything else than life's necessities. Deekie told Clay to let his brother have the new room. They would take over the loft that Truitt was vacating. Clay agreed, and this was the time of year Deekie never regretted their decision, for the newly added room did not benefit as much from the heat thrown off by the pot belly stove they also had added during the renovation of the old shack. The warmth rose up from the pot belly's hot metal surfaces like prayers offered from a pastor's altar to the heights of heaven. While she and her Virgil weren't quite the church-going types, they did believe in the graces bestowed on them by the Good Lord and were thankful for them, no matter how small. On these frigidly cold days of December, nothing was more heavenly than the climb up to the loft and into the warmth of the cabin bed she shared with her man.

Before she came to live with Virgil, her life had for too long been in need of a safe place to lay her head. Or a decent man to lay it down beside. The Lord's only denial to them had been children, despite all their trying. She had never discussed it with her Virgil, but Deekie hoped after one of their "*couplins*" it might bring forth something other than just mere pleasure. Their years together had been pleasant enough, but Deekie had recently been pining for a little one of her own. It just didn't come along naturally. So, she looked forward to having the gypsy's child to look after for a bit. Well, for four bits, actually, each and every day.

"Ya' can give them flecks to Alpheus when we git that gypsy baby later," she said. "And don't be fussin' with that death-riddled rag on the table we eat offa'."

"It won't hurt nuthin' none," Clay said, ignoring her. He carefully unwrapped the rag and soon found himself squinting hard at the white flecks blending in to the white cloth. White on white. He thought he might as well be pickin' cotton bolls after an early season snow.

"Alpheus don't like us callin' 'im by his Christian name, best to call 'im Sheriff Goff," Clay called out as she began to climb up to the loft. "Hey, Deeks, can ya' git me that mag'fyin' glass my Maw used to do her stitchin'."

"Dang it, Virgil," she protested as she stepped back down onto the floor of the large room that served as their kitchen, dining and living space. She walked over toward the dormant fireplace, which they would use only sparingly now that they had the potbelly, and rummaged through the basket he kept of his mother's things. These Clay would never allow her to sell off or throw out, and she knew better than to test him by doing so.

It's bad enough he has her planted jus' a short walk away in the field out back, she thought, *so as to pray over her grave most nights like he does. But he clings to her traps like she might come back and be in need of them one day. If she ever does, I swear I'll lay her low before he ever gits a chance to smile at her. Only fittin', nasty as she was to me durin' her lifetime.*

Deekie extracted several items from the basket and walked over with the glass and a small scrap of black felt.

"Here, Virgil," she said. "I don't need ya' strainin' yer eyes and losin' yer sight, too. Yer a burden 'nuff with jus' the one arm and yer bad hearin'. I knew yer mama saved this scrap of this dark material for somethin', so I reckon this must be it."

Deekie handed the black felt remnant to him as he wrestled to grasp the cotton cloth with just his one hand.

"That's perfect, Deeks," Clay said as she laid it on the table before him. "Since ya' done fussed about my missin' hand, why don't ya' hold this spit rag jus' so."

Deekie was always ribbing her man about his wound from the Battle of Chickamauga, but rarely in front of anyone else other than Truitt.

She used both her hands to stretch the cotton cloth taut over the black felt as Clay had asked. He then scraped its vertical surface with the blade of his pocket knife. Small white flakes appeared on the black felt surface as if coal miners had just accidentally tapped into a vein of salt.

"Look at all that stuff fallin' like dandruff on the shoulders of a preacher man's fancy black longcoat."

"Girl," Clay said, "ya' got some 'magination in that pretty li'l head of yours."

"Well, Virgil," she answered, "a girl's gotta have somethin' to make her life a li'l colorful."

"Well, speakin' of *kellerful*, this one speck ain't white like all the others." Clay used the tip of his knife blade to pick up the lone colorless blob - a tiny shard, not flat like the others. He held it up carefully to the flames of fire dancing between the air slits of the stove's belly. The wayward speck began to glisten as he did so. He moved the blade's tip and squinted with his bare eyes, not having a second hand to hold the magnifying glass.

"I think this might could be a real small piece of glass, Deeks. Put that cotton spit rag down and come take a close look for me."

She did so, as she picked up the magnifying glass. Deekie held it to her eye and soon she agreed with her man's observation. Its tiny, but jagged edges reflected the lively dancing flames.

"Even as small as it is, it still catches the flicker of them flames. What ya' figure it means?"

"I don't know," Clay said, "but it could be a clue as to why Miss Margaret's head wound was tore up the way it was. I gotta let Sheriff Goff know about this right away. Where's my coat?"

"Ya' draped it over that gypsy girl, 'member?" Deekie said sourly.

"I know that," Clay said, "but I got a heavier wool field coat for the thick of winter. Can ya' fetch it fer me?"

"Ah, hell, I might as well. I ain't gonna be able to git no sleep in the daylight now, not with everythin' goin' on. Give me a minute and I'll grab it fer ya'. I'll go along with ya' and I'll take hold of that gypsy chil'."

"Why did y'even agree to that?" Clay said. "Do ya' know what a pain havin'a baby around is gonna be fer all of us."

"I took it fer the four bits a day that comes along wit' it, Virgil. That's a good bit of money."

"And what do ya' need all that money fer, anyway?" Clay asked.

"I always wanted to have a real gussied up Christmas fer once under the roof of this house, with a tree and popcorn garland and silver strands of tinsel. Like all them proper town folks do it up. Besides, I got my eye on a special Christmas present fer ya', y'oaf."

Clay took his glance away from the speck on his knife's tip and turned it to her.

"How many years have we had Christmas together wit' no gifts other than each other's company?" Clay asked. "No, girl, y'are my blessin' from God Almighty. I don't need no other presents, Deeks."

"Nobody needs presents, Virgil. That's what makes 'em so special. It's somethin' nice that ya' might like, but definitely don't need. And they're given by someone who loves ya' most…"

"So what is this thing I don't need?"

"Could be, Virgil, a pair of nice leather gloves, but then ya'd only be in half need of 'em, wouldn't ya'? Or a nice new set of clean cotton spit rags."

"I certainly don't need 'em, Deeks. I barely use this one I got. I enjoy spittin' at things. I'm a pretty good aim."

"Yeah, so I seen," Deekie said. "They don't call ya' the *Sharpspitter of Sharpsburg* for nuthin'. Anyway, I'll tell ya' what yer gift is, iffen ya' must know. It's a … it's a…."

"It's a what?" Clay bit on her tease

"It's a secret, ya' knucklehead, so stop askin'."

Chapter Seven

Horse Trading for a Baby

When Clay and Deekie walked into the Sheriff's office, Goff was at his desk. The gypsy girl was behind him in the center of the jailhouse's three cells. She was dozing on the cot with her baby sleeping peacefully in her arms.

Sheriff Goff looked up at them and immediately raised his finger upright over his lips, warning them to be quiet.

"Don't make no noise," he whispered. "Damn if she didn't jus' git that squawkin' bundle of lungs asleep."

He jerked his head to the cell behind him. The look on his face said there'd be hell to pay if anyone disturbed his newfound and highly cherished peace.

Clay closed the door as gently as he could behind Deekie, choking out the brisk December morning air.

In a soft voice he asked, "Where's Miss Margaret?"

"In heaven, I pray," the sheriff said softly with a wry smirk, "but her earthly remains are over at the undertaker's. Why do y'ask? If ya' got questions fer her, she ain't takin' none no more."

Clay drew the black felt from inside his coat. "Well, before she gits thrown in a grave, ya' might ask that undertaker to go over her real close lookin' fer bits of glass."

Clay used his thumb to open up the piece of black felt. As he did, Deekie drifted back toward the jail cell behind the sheriff's desk. She stood silently and watched over the small child resting so comfortably on the bosom of its mama. She wondered just how peaceful that must feel.

"I found what I reckon' to be a small piece of glass," Clay said softly. "in amongst them white specks I scraped from that dead stray's tongue."

Clay laid the felt flat on the desk and extracted his pocket knife. He then carefully lifted the transparent speck on its tip.

"Is that so?" Goff seemed interested. "That's awful small. How ya' figure it to be glass?"

"It caught the flicker of the flames in our stove. Ya' might want to have that undertaker check Miss Margaret's hair and scalp right close. I figure maybe she was struck with a bottle that broke 'part and sliced her head open."

Goff lowered his own voice, as it had been growing in volume with his excitement. "Yeah, Clay, I think I'll do that. It might explain her forehead bein' tore up the way we found her. Ya' stay here with Deekie and our prisoners, I'll walk over to the undertaker's office right now."

Sheriff Goff got up as quietly as he could from his desk, but one leg of the chair scraped across the hardwood planks of the floor. He shuddered his shoulders, as if fearful of the baby waking. But no cry was forthcoming from the infant. Its rest remained undisturbed.

"Shush now, Sheriff!" Deekie whispered sternly.

"No harm done," the sheriff whispered quietly in response as he made his way to the door.

When the door closed behind him, Deekie moved over to his desk, which Clay stood beside as still as death itself. He seemed afraid for his life to make any sound at all, and Deekie spotted the rare presence of fear in his eyes.

She settled herself down gently into the wooden chair, and lifted it ever so slightly to pull herself up to the blotter. She peered over the desk hoping to eye any report of a crime or other secretive document, but none was to be found. However, what she saw on the edge of the desk caught her attention and she reached for it.

"Y'ought not be touchin' nuthin!" Clay whispered.

"Relax, Virgil," she said softly as she picked up the newsprint on the edge of the desk. "It's just the Cartersville newspaper, silly. I don't reckon Alpheus would mind me 'musin' myself with it."

A befuddled look overtook Clay. He was searchin' his mind for something to say in response and seemed to have gotten lost somewhere in its depths.

"I thought the Cartersville paper done went out of business earlier this year" he said in the softest tone as he could muster.

"Well, it did, sort of," Deekie replied in an equally soft voice, "but that was the *Cartersville Standard and Express.* This here is the first edition of the new *Cartersville Express,* says so right here."

Deekie held up the front page and read from the large open block notice on its left hand side.

"Says here *'The Express by C.H.C. Willingham'* and jus' below it, *'The Old Standard and Express.'* It will come out every Thursday from here on out."

'Well, I'll be. So what's the news around town?"

"Cotton sales, mostly," Deekie said. "An article 'bout Southern iron, even an advertisement by J.J. Howard that his cotton gin is up and runnin'."

"Well, I guess next week Mr. Willin'ham will have sumthin' jus' a little more excitin' to print, I mean with the murder of Miss Margaret, won't he?"

"Sons of bitches!" Deekie said aloud in a startled voice as she slapped her palm on the sheriff's desk. It caught Clay off guard, as her voice was loud enough to raise Miss Margaret, let alone the rest of the dead and the sleepin' baby in the cell behind them.

"What?" Clay asked. No answer came right off.

"It weren't nuthin', Virgil," she said finally as she continued to search the paper's front page.

"It had to be somethin'," Clay said, "as ya' nearly woke that gypsy child up. Thank God it didn't stir none."

"Jus' says here," she said falsely explaining her outburst, "that the editors of the Baltimore Sun newspaper is criticizin' the local politicians who are askin' for federal assistance with their plans to dig the Coosa Canal to connect the Alabama and Tennessee Rivers." 9

"And that caused ya' to stir the way ya' done?" Clay asked, somewhat in disbelief.

---

9 The story of the Baltimore Sun commenting on the Coosa Canal, as well as the articles on Cotton Sales, and Southern Iron were all featured on the front page of the premier issue of "The Cartersville Express" issued on December 2nd, 1875.

"It's jus' them showboats up in Maryland think they're so special. Ya' know a lot of the local families with money down here send their young girls up there for proper schoolin' in Baltimore? They call it finishin' school. Up there they got what's called the Peabody Institute complete with a full symphony. *Real Lah-Tee-Dah!"*

Deekie was laying it on thick, but only to cover her real surprise. She knew her protest of the high living folks, especially those up North, would ring true with her man. But in reality, her shock had been from the last announcement in the lower right hand column of the front page that read:

John T. Owen

At Sayre & Co. Drug Store,

Main Street,

Will sell watches, clocks and Jewelry, Spectacles, Silver and Silver Plated Goods as cheap as they can be bought anywhere. Warranted to prove as represented. All work done by me warranted to give satisfaction. Give me a call. [10]

The advertisement was for the very stand within that drug store where Deekie had spotted the present she intended to buy for her Virgil. And there was only one of the items she wanted left. She hadn't the money to buy it when she saw it, but now she feared someone would see this notice, be drawn there and beat her to it. She knew she had to buy the item as fast as possible, but to do so would mean needing to get her hands on some cash, and quick.

---

[10] Verbatim re-creation of actual advertisement, The Cartersville Express, December 2, 1875.

Clay thought his woman seemed to pout after that. He knew better than to fuss over her too much when she got this way. Best to leave her be, even if it meant that an awkward silence would raise up between them. So they shared in its quiet until the sheriff returned.

"I can't do it, Sheriff!" Deekie yelled out at him as he came through the door, catching Goff off guard and causing him to slam the door in response. The infant immediately exploded into a wail that pierced the office and awoke the child's mother.

"Damn it, Deekie!" Goff said in anger. "Why ya' gotta go and scream at me like that. Thank God yer takin' that child wit' ya."

"No, I am not," she said in protest. "That's what I can't do, Alpheus."

Goff looked at Clay who could only shrug his shoulders.

"We got a deal," Goff said, "and it's Sheriff Goff, not Alpheus to you."

"We got no deal, Sheriff," Deekie said. "I never signed nuthin'. It's a free country, after all."

The gypsy baby would not stop crying as Sheriff Goff attempted to understand exactly what had changed since he left. "Come now, Deekie, I can't pay ya' any more than half dollar a day. Stop tryin to run me up, gal."

"Then pay me in advance for two weeks and I'll consider it," she rebutted briskly.

"That would be five dollars," Goff said. "I don't have five dollars in petty cash jus' lyin' around here in the office. I can't believe ya'd even think I did."

"Fine," Deekie said, "then our deal's off, Sheriff."

"I'll pay ya' every Thursday for the comin' week," he responded, surrendering to her slyly having pinned him down in a financial negotiation ambush.

"Startin' today!" Deekie insisted! "Yer puttin' two and a half dollars in my palm right here and that will cement our deal, with God and Virgil as our witnesses."

The child's whines grew all the louder as Deekie spoke as loudly and aggressively as she could.

"Alright, already," Sheriff Goff said. "Git yer backside outta my chair so I can get yer bribe, I mean advance, outta my petty cash safe."

Deekie got up and watched as Goff made his way around Clay to his chair. Before he accessed his drawer with his petty cash container in it, he shooed both Clay and Deekie to the other side of the desk. Then he took a key hanging amongst several others from his belt, opened the cash box and extracted two and a half dollars in coins. He offered them to Deekie who stood across the desk still with her arms folded.

"There's one more thing," she insisted.

"Of course there is," Sheriff Goff said, "it couldn't possibly be this easy jus' to give ya' what y'asked fer."

"Every Thursday," Deekie said over the baby's wailing, "ya' will pay me for the comin' week in full, mine to keep even if my duties end before the week does."

"Agreed," said the sheriff stiffly.

"And ya' will give me this every week as well," she said holding up the Cartersville Express.

"And what else?" Goff asked.

Deekie hesitated for effect before finally saying, "Nothin', that's it."

The sheriff put the coins in her palm, and finally snapped, "Now let's git that child outta here."

As he turned to open up the cell, he heard the office door open and Deekie cry out as she ran out, "I jus' gotta take care of somethin' first and I'll be right back fer the baby…"

The door slammed as the sheriff turned around in shock. "What in Betty's blue blazes was that?"

Clay looked at the sheriff. "I could have warned ya' not to dicker with her. She drives a hard bargain."

"She'll drive ya' to a lot more than that," Sheriff Goff warned as he watched Deekie walk briskly across the iron rails of the Western and Atlantic Rail Road tracks and make her way toward Main Street.

Chapter Eight

The World in Her Hand

Deekie walked down to Sayre's Drug Store not far the railroad tracks on Main Street. As she walked into the storefront from the cold December air, her palm still wrapped tightly around the most money she had ever held, save for the cash she and Clay were to supposed to bring home from Texas before his *Diddy* ran off with it all. Thank God for the reward Colonel Tumlin's lawyers wrestled out of the Texans later, or they would have been in some dire straits.

"Well, Miss Deekie," a full voice boomed out, "What a pleasure to see you again. This time I see you left your six-shooter at home."

The voice belonged to the gregarious John T. Owen who manned a set of beautifully lacquered hardwood and spotless glass cabinet cases full of various niceties for sale.

"Well, to tell ya' true," she said, "Sheriff Goff ain't too fond of me carryin' it 'round town. So when I have business wit' him, I tend to leave it at home."

"Of course, of course," the businessman said. "What can I do for you this fine day?"

Deekie pointed to an artifact in the display case.

"I'm in need of seein' that fancy glass ball again," she said. "The one with the tiny snowy village inside it."

"Ah, the *Schneekugel!*" He said, emphasizing the foreign pronunciation as he reached into the case for the requested item.

"The what?" she asked.

"That's German for *'Snow Globe.'* I have these shipped in all the way from Vienna, Austria." Owen shook the globe in his hand for effect, kicking up a placid snowfall within it. "So far as I know, this is the only place in the state where you can purchase one. As I told you when you were here last, this is the last one I currently have for sale, although just this morning I had a woman ride the trains all the way up from Atlanta just to come and see it. I expect her back tomorrow to purchase it. However, I am expecting another shipment in, just after the holidays."

"That won't do me no good," Deekie said. "Let me see that snow globe, please."

"Well, Miss Deekie," Owen said, "I have to limit how much this delicate item is handled. I would hate to have someone shake it too vigorously only to have it drop and break. And as I told you on your last visit, it is very expensive at two full dollars and a half, but that is because of the many hours of old world craftsmanship put into it."

Deekie slammed her palm down on the top glass of the cabinet just above a row of silver-plated pocket watches. She smiled as Mr. Owen's eyes opened wide with his hearing the sound of three large coins hit the glass beneath her flattened hand. She raised her hand away slowly, revealing two silver trade dollar pieces and a half-dollar coin to boot.

"Does this buy me the right to hold it?" she asked.

"It most certainly does," the businessman replied, with a wry smile spreading across his face.

Deekie left the coins on the glass counter and took hold of the snow globe. She gave it a fresh shake and watched the snow swirl over the village in a thick slurry of transparent fluid, not settling out very quickly at all, but remaining semi-suspended over the enclosed town, as if by some magical spell.

She became transfixed watching the snow slowly settle. "It's like holdin' the world in yer hand."

"So you'd like to *procure* it, I presume," Owen said.

"I dunno," she said, "the third little wooden roof in this alpine village has a weird shaped chip missin' from its corner. I guess that was what made ya' leery to have folk handlin' it in the first place."

"It is precisely the reason for my concern," Mr. Owen said. "Regrettably, it is the only one I have left, as I have already said. So are you interested in taking it home with you?"

"No, but I will pay ya' fer it," Deekie replied.

"I don't understand," said the businessman, honestly not making sense of the words she was saying.

"I'll buy it, but I can't take it with me as my Virgil is waitin' fer me in Sheriff Goff's office," Deekie explained. "It is a Christmas gift fer him. I will pay ya' full, here and now, and return to pick it up when I am alone. Is that okay with ya'?"

"That is quite acceptable," Owen agreed.

"But, iffen ya' was to go and sell it out from under me to some rich train ridin' hussy from Atlanta," Deekie said sternly, "well, in that case I am prone to return to this here store with my Navy Six and give ya' a demonstration of jus' how accurately it can be fired."

"No, Miss Deekie, once our sale is concluded," Owen assured her with a laugh, "nothing could keep this item from you. I have my professional ethics to uphold."

Owen reached for the coins, prompting Deekie to grab out with her free hand to take his by the wrist. She then looked him in the eye and said, "Whoa there, Mr. Owen. Leave that half dollar where it lies. I don't figure to pay full price for this item with the roof chipped as it is."

She rotated the globe in her other hand such that her thumb pointed up at the slight defect in the wooden village scene. Then, after she saw Owen's eyes focus on it, she gave the snow globe another good shake. As she did she thought, *My Virgil will love this come Christmas morn.*

"Miss Deekie," Owen replied to her offer, "the product's price is sadly not negotiable."

"Mr. Owen," she replied, "I think yer old 'nuff to realize that everythin' in this here life is negotiable. Ya' can split that fifty cent loss with the item's maker. Or ya' can keep yer dinged-up snow globe and hope that train ridin' hussy from Atlanta comes back to pay full price. But ifffen she was real, and I doubt even that she is, she'd have bought it while she was here, and not have to invest in the cost of another Western & Atlantic Railroad roundtrip fare jus' to come back and *procure* it."

She intentionally over-pronounced the word *"procure"* in the same high-faluting manner he had earlier.

Deekie eventually handed the snow globe back to the proprietor, and then flatly said, "Deal or no deal at two full trade dollars[11] and not a penny more?"

John T. Owen thought on the recent slow sales, and decided to take the bird-in-hand offer.

Deekie received a receipt for the transaction, and reclaimed her fifty cent piece. She then moved over to the drug store counter and asked the pharmacist about a feeding vessel for the infant.

"Well, Miss Deekie," said the pharmacist, "looks like you come to exactly the right place. We recently procured a line of all glass baby bottles with Indian rubber nipples from Philadelphia. Also, should you need it, we are now carrying that Sweetened Condensed Milk made by Mr. Gail Borden out of New York. A lot of people in town have taken to using it for baby food. The bottles are a half dollar each, and the cans of Eagle Milk are 30 cents each."

"Milk in cans?"

"Sure nuff?

"How's come it don't spoil?"

"Because it's evaporated," explained the druggist. "Word has it that this Mr. Borden was on a ship returning from Europe. The ship had two cows aboard for fresh milk. The cows got sick at sea and died, and the contaminated milk sickened and killed some children on board. Mr. Borden is an inventor type and developed the evaporating process so the milk can be canned and will stay fresh. The babies like it cause it's sweetened with syrup. Borden sold a ton of it to the Union Army during the war. He's a real stickler for cleanliness in his factory and dairies."

---

[11] Trade dollars were silver dollar coins minted primarily for trade with external countries such as China at that time. Despite their foreign intent, Trade Dollars were used within the states given the economic distress caused by the Coinage Act of 1873.

"That Borden fella is right proud of his product," Deekie said. "So proud that I can't afford it none. Besides, nothin' that fed the Union Army is comin' under my roof, I can assure ya' that. I will take the bottle, but I also need a dozen of them cloth diapers and some diaper pins."

"Okie-doke," the druggist said with a warm smile. "That will be one dollar even."

"But I only got fifty cents. Can I give ya' the other fifty cents come next Thursday?"

"Sure," the druggist said flatly, his warm smile evaporated away like his canned milk, "and I'll give you the bottle now and the diapers and pins next week."

"But I need them now too," she answered. "Can't feed a child and not expect business at the other end…"

"And I'll need one full dollar now," he replied.

"Look," Deekie argued, "this is official sheriff's business. Sheriff Goff will vouch for me makin' good on the other fifty cent. I swear by Virgil's Maw in the grave."

"Don't you go swearing in my place of business, young lady," the druggist said. "I'll tell you what - I'll give you all the goods today, but if you're lying about Sheriff Goff vouching for you, I will have Mr. Owen deny you that snow globe you just bought from him. Yeah, I heard your whole conversation with him. As of now, that snow globe is what the finance types would call collateral until you pay me my fifty cents owed."

"I think I'm offended," said Deekie.

"What, at not being trusted for the four bits?"

"No," she replied, "for bein' called a young lady. That's a name no one ever done laid on me before."

Chapter Nine

A Life in Her Hand

The wailing had stopped by the time Deekie walked back into Sheriff Goff's office, but only because the gypsy had silenced the child by feeding it. Unlike his younger brother earlier that morning, her Virgil had turned his back and refused to look. The sheriff could not care less so long as the act brought quiet back to the office.

"Okay, Deekie," Goff said, "A deal is a deal."

"Yer right, sheriff, a deal is a deal," Deekie agreed. "But ya' best vouch for me over at Sayre's Drug Store. I used my last fifty cents to buy this feedin' bottle for the chil', but I still owe them that much more for the diapers and pins. Here, take half to keep for when the chil's here."

"What did ya' do with the other two dollars I jus' give ya'?" The lawman said.

"Never ya' mind," she snapped at him. "That was my money the minute ya' laid it in my palm, and I don't in no way have to answer to ya' for how I spend it."

"Then I don't have to vouch for ya' that yer good for the rest of it," Goff snapped back.

"Fine then, Sheriff Goff," Deekie said. "Then ya' go ahead and keep this wailin' baby with its Mama. Ain't no skin off my nose, is it?"

"No, ya' done took my money and yer takin' that baby, sure as a month full of Sundays. If I gotta vouch for ya', then against my better judgement, I will, but yer not leavin' here without this little one."

With that she followed Goff over to the cell, where the sheriff unlocked the cell door and opened it wide. The gypsy mother nursed the child as he did so, looking up with large swollen eyes that seemed to understand somehow exactly what was about to transpire. The open cell door did not mean her freedom, but she appeared content in knowing it meant freedom for her child.

After the child was fed, the mother covered herself and tended to the infant until it was burped. Then, the gypsy held out the child to Deekie, who sensed that she had somehow developed a bond with the woman during their few hours together the night before. This gypsy mother appeared to trust her, but Deekie could not understand quite why. Maybe just because while the gypsy mother couldn't understand the words, somehow she had realized that it was Deekie who talked the deputy into letting her out of that jail cell to go off and find her unattended baby.

Deekie reached in to take the infant, but as she did, the mother gently grasped her wrist and slid her palm down over the back of Deekie's hand. As she did this, something resembling a mild shock ran through her being.

Deekie instantly had a vision of herself nursing a child. This child? She could not be sure. Still, while this image flashed through her mind, she could feel a tender closeness to the baby that she could never have imagined. *What had this gypsy Mama done to her? Was this a blessing or a curse of some sort?*

That feeling, the vision as it was, left her as quickly as it had come over her. She stood above the gypsy mother, who released the grasp of her hand, for the first time leaving her child alone in Deekie's arms. The woman's eyes looked up plaintively at Deekie, expressing a sorrow that the gypsy somehow knew was unavoidable. The child could not stay in this drafty jail cell, as she must. It must be protected and nurtured. Her eyes screamed out to Deekie, *take my child, but more importantly, take care of my child.*

Shortly thereafter, Clay and Deekie took the child wrapped in a blanket for the mile long walk to their home. Up along Market Street until it merged with the Mission Trail and then down the hill and across the rough hewn bridge laid over Pettit's Creek to their homestead. The whole time, the infant cried for its mother.

"Didn't Zach Harper's wife pass in childbirth?" Deekie asked Clay as they passed the Harper spread.

"Yeah, but that was year's ago, Deeks," Clay answered. "His boy must be three years old by now."

"Well," she said, "I never thought on it for a second 'fore, but with his wife dyin', jus' how did he feed that baby? Maybe ya' need to stop in and see him, get some knowin' on how we should feed this child. Jus' 'nuff until the sheriff has deputy Howard bring the gypsy down tomorra' to feed it."

"I can do that," Clay said, "But let's git ya' home first. This chil' needs to get on out of this cold. Last thing we need is for the baby to get sick and die on us."

So they walked past the Harper property and to their own, just a short hike further down the Mission Trail.

Chapter Ten

You Can Lead a Child to Milk

The icy draft cut through the warm cabin just as sharply as it's total opposite - that being a hot knife through cold hard butter. Its frigid chill made Deekie aware of her Virgil's return from the Harper spread.

"It's 'bout time yer got back, Virgil. This chil' hasn't caught half a breath since we left Sheriff Goff's office," she called out over the hungry baby's wailing.

"I know. I could hear the poor thing as I come on up the trail to the cabin. Sounds like some kind of wounded animal with a leg caught in a trap."

"Well, what did Zach tell ya'?"

"Most all we need to know, I figure," Clay answered, as he closed the cabin door and began taking off his woolen winter overcoat. "Mos' 'mportant was not to give the child cow's milk. Too harsh for their young bellies to break down. Best food he found for his boy was goat's milk. Said Doc Hardin was the one who said so when his wife passed jus' after givin' birth to Wade."

"Goat's milk? Huh?" Deekie repeated with surprise.

"Zach said he raised Wade on it with no real problems a't'all," Clay added. "Supposed to be the closest animal's milk to a mother's own."

"Where on earth are we goin' to get fresh goat milk?" Deekie asked.

"From the front porch, I reckon. Zach gave us a big glass jar full of it. I carried it home with me, but left it out there in the cold. He still milks them goats to this day for his boy. I guess his Wade done worked up somethin' of a taste for it. Zach tol' me to stop by whenever it is we might find ourselves in need o' more."

"Ya' gotta do anything to it?" she asks.

"Zach says best to stir some cane sugar syrup into it," he answered, "jus' nuff to sweeten it up a bit. He also said it'd be best to smear some on whatever ya' decide to use as a nipple."

"I'm a might curious now. What did Ol' Zach use to feed that goat milk to his baby boy?"

"A hollowed out bull's horn with a bunched up linen cloth on the end as a sort o' teat. He showed it to me. Tol' me to take it, if I liked, but I tol' him ya' had bought one of them new glass baby bottles with the Injun rubber nipples from the drug store. Zach said they didn't even have them here in town only a few years ago."

"Well, I reckon them to be purdy new," Deekie said. "That druggist said they jus' come in, along with that condensed Eagle Brand milk he was so quick to try and sell me. Zach say anythin' else?"

"Oh, yeah, Zach said be sure to keep everythin' clean as a whistle, or that baby can get sick as sin. He said he would scald that bull horn in boilin' water after every time he used it."

"That's a stupid sayin'" Deekie snipped.

"What?"

"Clean as a whistle," she said. "Whistles have all that spittle and such in them, they ain't clean a't'all."

"It's jus' a sayin', Deeks," Clay said, tryin' to focus her. "Important thing is to keep everythin' clean."

"Well, we sure can do that," she said. "We'll jus' keep a pot of water 'top the pot belly. I reckon that Injun rubber nipple can take the heat alright."

The baby's crying cut through her last few words to the point Clay had to struggle to make out her meaning.

"Well, Virgil, let's git to it. The bottle's on the table. Fill it up. And bring me the cane sugar syrup from the cupboard, I'll mix it in."

"Sure," Clay said as he moved toward the porch, "but tell me, did y'ever figure if that's a little boy or a little girl we're dealin' with?"

"Don't right matter when they're hungry, Virgil."

"I know," he said with a look on his face that said for her not to be so quick with him, " but jus' like y'are, I'm a might curious too, that's all."

"Well, while ya' was at Zach's spread gittin' the goat's milk, I had to change her diaper," Deekie said, "and there ain't no doubt she's a li'l missy all right. She can't be more than six or seven month's old."

"That raises 'nuther matter," Clay said. "What are we gonna call her? Can only say that *child* for so long…"

"Will ya' jus' git that goat's milk from the porch," Deekie snapped at him, "instead of standin' there playin' a game of twunny questions."

With that said, Clay took the bottle outside onto the cold porch. He filled it by sitting on the stump they kept for chopping firewood on and holding the bottle in between his knees. He then used his hand to pour enough goat's milk out to near fill it up. He took it in to Deekie, then grabbed the cane syrup. She then swirled in a drizzle of the syrup, and even passed the rubber nipple under its stream as Zach had suggested.

"So, what *are* we gonna call her?" Clay repeated.

"Grab me that book I borro'd from Miss Margaret's house."

"Ya' mean stole," Clay ribbed her. "Truitt done tol' me what ya' done."

"I'm jus' gonna read it and take it back," she said. "Borro'd. I ain't gonna wear them words off the pages none. Borro'd, not stole."

Clay grabbed the book from off the mantle of the fireplace. He could feel the richness of its thick brown leather cover that stretched across its spine. "I don't know, Deeks. Ya' get awful attached to things."

Deekie held the wriggling infant in the crook of her left arm as she raised the bottle with her right hand. But every time she pushed the nipple to the mouth of the infant, the child just turned her head away.

"Come on now," Deekie said softly to the child, "we both know ya' to be starvin', so go on and take this Injun rubber nipple in yer mouth. Ya' got somethin' against Injuns? Or jus' the taste of rubber?"

The baby resisted, for as restless as she was, she would not take the strange hard nipple into her mouth.

"Virgil, open that book up and look through it until yer see a character's name that starts with an 'E.' She's s'posed to be a beautiful gypsy girl. That's why I took that book, I knew it had gypsy stuff in it. Keep lookin' till ya' find that name used over and over again. That's what we're gonna call this little gal."

"Ya' done took it before y'ever knew it had gypsies in it," Clay argued with her. "Y'only took it cause it had them Edgar Allan Poe lookin' gargoyles drawn in it."

"Jus' look fer the name I tol' ya' to…"

Clay read through the book, or more accurately he looked through it. The sheer number of words intimidated him something fierce. He never really tried to read anything; instead he just sort of spot searched for a repeated name starting with an 'E.' He turned the pages until he came to it's sixth chapter.

"Here's a name startin' with an E. It's in here a lot. E-S-M-E-R-A-L…"

"That's it, Esmeralda, that's such a pretty name."

"It's pretty alright, but it's a mouthful," Clay said. "A man could wear his jaw down to a nub sayin' all that every time he spoke of his chil'."

Deekie wrestled with the child that still refused to take the nipple into her mouth. She arched her back and kicked defiantly.

"Well, then, we'll jus' have to call this little wiggle worm Miss Essie, won't we?"

"Essie," Clay let the sound roll off his tongue. "That's easy 'nuff to get out. Yeah, I'm already takin' favor with it. So, Essie it is."

Essie cried out louder than she had been since leaving the town square. Deekie ran her finger over the little girl's fat chubby cheek, when an idea popped into her head. She traced her finger through the syrup on the nipple of the bottle and held it to the baby's mouth. Miss Essie turned her head away, but Deekie then smeared the tiniest bit of the sweet syrup she could on the baby's lower lip.

"I'll be damned if this baby will go hungry much longer," Deekie said. "I'm eager to read that book, and that ain't 'bout to happen 'til this baby eats and then sleeps a bit. Come to think of it I could use a bit of sleep myself, after bein' up all night 'cause of you, Virgil."

"She jus' licked that syrup off her lip, Deeks," he said, ignoring her accusation. Deekie looked down to see the baby licking again at her lip, and held her sticky finger up to Miss Essie's face. Slowly pushing it forward, the baby's delicate tongue, nothing larger than a tiny red speck, licked at the syrup again. But when Deekie next raised the rubber nipple to the baby's mouth, even though it was coated with a thin veneer of cane sugar syrup, the child turned her head away.

"Come on, Essie, take that nipple and eat, will ya?" Deekie said in an unusually sweet tone for her.

"I guess she don't know what to make of the Injun rubber thing," Clay said. "She ain't never seen one before, don't know what it's fer."

Deekie instantly looked up at her man with a smile.

"That might be the smartest thing ya' said in a long while, Virgil," Deekie said as she returned the sweetened finger to the baby's mouth. She could feel the softest pull of the baby sucking on its tip. "Ya' done give me an idea."

With that Deekie started to undo the top of her dress, slipping one shoulder out of it. She reached across with her free hand and cupped her young breast that hung bare. She then traced her finger over her own nipple.

"What are ya' doin'?" Clay asked. "Ain't nuthin' in that to feed her with."

"She jus' needs to learn what that that taste means," she said and raised the child to her nearly bare nipple, a thin film of cane sugar syrup being its only covering. "She already knows what a teat is fer. If she learns that teats are sweet, then maybe that next sweet thing she tastes she'll reckon to be a teat too. Come on, Miss Essie…"

She held the child's face to her breast. After a bit, the baby took Deekie's nipple to her mouth. A few minutes later, sure enough, the child began sucking on the natural nipple, but, of course, was not rewarded with any milk.

Deekie then removed her and tried again to insert the rubber nipple into the child's mouth without success. Then she would return Miss Essie to her breast, but each time she pulled her away to return to the rubber nipple the child fussed. Still, Deekie was determined, and kept this cycle up over the next few hours. With no results to show for her efforts, this aggravated the weary woman to no end.

Deekie stayed in the chair with Essie as Clay kept his vigil watching over them. When Deekie finally gave into her exhaustion and nodded off, Clay stayed close to make sure the infant didn't somehow wriggle free and fall. He was infatuated with how small and dependent the child was on them both, not just for its survival, but for the human touch and nurturing they would provide.

Li'l Miss Essie was gonna be theirs for a bit.

While Deekie slept he thought on how low the gypsy mother in the jail cell must be feeling. Still, she must have, in some way, known how well his Deeks would look after her daughter. After all, she gave up her child willingly to them. Then Clay wondered if the mother even understood she was being held for the murder of Miss Margaret. He could see nothing in her that would suggest violence of that kind, but kept telling himself that emotions and fear were a powerful thing. Under their influence, people been known to do some terrible things they never thought they could be capable of. He remembered his first kill during the war, how scared he was before he done it, and how ever more scared he was afterward knowing he had that capacity within his natural make-up.

Deekie slept in the chair for less than a half hour in total, but that little bit of sleep refreshed her in a most satisfying way. She panicked when she remembered the baby. She came out of her drowse in a disoriented fog, fearing for half a second she had dropped the poor thing. She arched her back and felt the infant's weight upon her bosom, but when her eyes traced down to it, she was shocked at what she saw. Miss Essie was sucking on the Indian rubber nipple, and must have been for a while as a good bit of the bottle was now empty.

"That's it, Miss Essie," she said to the little girl, "yer sharp as a tack, aren't ya'? Just wanted to take that thing on yer own terms. I don't blame ya' a bit."

"She's been suckin' on that rubber nipple since ya' done drifted off," Clay said. "It's right peaceful jus' sittin' here watchin' her draw that bottle down."

"Virgil, she's so sweet," Deekie said, "like the li'l girl we never been able to have."

"Now, Deeks," he said stiffly, "don't ya' go gittin' too attached to her. This is only temp'rary, 'member that. That child has to go back to its mama."

Deekie raised her head and Clay feared what she might say next. When the words came, they were edged with the sharpest barbs of reality.

"That's if she still has a mama to go back to after all is said and done 'bout Miss Margaret's murder. Maybe we'll git the chance to raise Miss Essie as our own after all."

Clay gave his woman a snarling look. "Don't ya' go wishin' nothin' ill on that gypsy woman, Deeks. The Lord don't look kindly on that. Don't covet thy neighbor's children."

"Shame on ya', Virgil" Deekie snapped. "I don't wish no ill on her. Her future is in the hands of the Lord and the law. I'll let Him and the courts decide her fate. I'm jus' sayin' if all goes against her, someone will have to raise this baby. So, why not us?"

Chapter Eleven

News of the Hun

Truitt returned home from his work at the courthouse that night excited as a fox cornered by a pack of yapping hounds. His face was flush, and his brow arched in such a way that Clay knew he came bearing news, and that it was not likely to be news that Deekie would want to hear.

"Clay," Truitt said, straining to keep out of Deekie's earshot, "Yer not going to believe this. That German fella' Schilling came in to see Judge Ferris in his chambers this afternoon."

"Why? What could he be wantin' from the judge?"

"That's what I wanted to know," Truitt said, "so I made up a fuss to interrupt them so Judge Ferris could sign some court documents. They coulda' waited, but I was nosin' around a bit."

"Well," Clay asked, "what were they talkin' bout?"

"Ya' see, that German got quiet after I walked in," Truitt said, "but the judge is used to me intrudin' so, and he jus' kept on talkin' in response to Schilling's questions. Sounded like Schilling was asking if Miss Margaret's property would be sold on the courthouse steps once the gypsy is found guilty of murdering Miss Margaret."

"Well, that could mean either he really wants to get a crack at her land and home borderin' his," Clay said, "or he was jus' feelin' out the judge on whether that gypsy woman would be brought to trial on murder charges."

"I think it well might be the latter," Truitt confessed, "cause after I left I lingered a bit outside his chambers. The judge was sayin' how the process has to be allowed to play out. Schilling said something to him in German, but the Judge had to ask him what it meant. Schilling explained it was something like, *the devil's favorite piece of furniture is the long bench.* When Judge Ferris asked what that meant, Schilling told him the long bench was where craftsmen would put work they figured they would put off 'til later."

"Sort of meanin' like don't put off til tomorrow what ya' can do today. I git it. Why would Schilling be in such a hurry to bring that girl to trial?"

"Well, from what ya' said about last night, Clay," Truitt reasoned, "It sounded like he was tryin' his best to agitate that crowd into takin' action against her. Thank God ya' were there to make sure no such thing happened."

"Thing is Truitt," Clay said, "Schilling is acting a might odd, iffen y'ask me. If the gypsy girl done it, it'll come out in court. Why push so hard to rush the case…"

"*Expedite,* Clay, is what we call it in court."

"Okay, but why *exspite* it a't'all?" Clay didn't like the way this was all shapin' up. He didn't like his brother snoopin' round the judge's chamber door. He was lucky to keep his job after that business with Willet's dagger a few years back. Clay had to admit it sounded as though the German sure acted like a man who had something to hide. Most of all, the judge giving Schilling an ear worried Clay.

"Why expedite it? Maybe cause Schilling saw that gypsy smash in his neighbor's head," Deekie said, having listened in on their talk. "Could be he liked Miss Margaret and didn't take kindly to seein' her skull caved in."

"Whose side ya' on in this, Deeks?" Truitt clipped in a surprised but angry tone.

"I am on the side of the truth, Truitt," she said in response. "Ain't that how it's s'posed to work? And don't raise yer voice so. Miss Essie jus' got herself to sleep."

Just as they quarreled over this, a knock came at the door. Clay answered it, not knowing who it might be. When he opened up, there stood Sheriff Goff in the darkness, although the hour was not particularly late.

"Clay, I hope ya' don't mind me bargin' in on y'all at suppertime."

"No, Sheriff, we ain't sat down to table jus' yet. But we got plenty 'nuff to welcome ya' to join us."

"I appreciate that, but no, I'm here on sheriffin' business. I come to pass some news on to ya' and Miss Deekie. I received a writ late this afternoon from Judge Ferris keepin' me from sending that gypsy woman down here tomorrow as I said I would have Howard do to feed her youngin'. His order said she was a threat to the community and was prone to high-tail it off with the baby. She is not to be let out of the jail cell 'cept for exercise and necessities, if ya' git my gist."

"Sounds like Schilling's doin' to me," Clay said.

"Don't matter much now," Deekie chirped in, "cause we got Miss Essie feedin' proper from the bottle."

"Who's Miss Essie?" asked Goff.

"The youngin', ya' simple man," Deekie said disrespectfully. "And keep yer voice down Sheriff, she's asleep and I'd like to keep it that way. If she starts wailin', then yer takin' her with ya'."

"I tol' ya' not to get too attached to that chil', girl," Clay said. "We could be lookin' after her fer a long time, and yer already beginnin' to worry me."

"Don't fret too much," Sheriff Goff said, "cause Judge Ferris set a trial date for the gypsy woman in the week between Christmas and New Year."

"How did all this happen without me knowin'?" Truitt asked.

"I wondered why ya' didn't carry that writ over from the courthouse to my office," the Sheriff said. "Came late, jus' as I was closin' up the place. But I got a feeling the judge might jus' want to keep y'out of the middle of all this, Truitt, as ya' was there last night with us all."

"Especially if that German put a bug in his ear," Truit responded. "Maybe he did so after I walked in on them in his chamber."

"What will happen to Miss Essie if the gypsy is found guilty?" Deekie asked.

"That's up to the judge to decide," Sheriff Goff answered. "Often, it's not uncommon to find someone in the community to adopt a chil' that small. Or we might come to track down some of her kin."

"Really?" Deekie said, her pulse racing after hearing the words.

"Wait," Clay protested. "How can they put that woman on trial when she don't speak a lick of English?"

"That's the other thing," Goff said. "The Judge already telegraphed over to Franklin College and they got someone over there might be able to translate for her. A Dr. Stevens, professor of European languages. He's teachin' courses now, that's why the trial won't be until the week before New Years. The professor will be comin' in by train the day after Christmas."

"Jus' in time on St. Stephen's day," Truitt said.

"What?" asked the surprised Sheriff Goff.

"The day after Christmas is St. Stephen's feast day."

"How do y'even know that?" Sheriff Goff asked.

"Yeah, Truitt," Clay added, "Them saints are a Catholic bunch. Ya' sure ain't Catholic. Most nobody round here is."

"I bet that German is," Deekie added. "Lots of 'em are. I reckon he's right about that gypsy, though. She well coulda' done this…"

Clay cut her a silencing look, then asked his brother, "So, Truitt, how y'even know 'bout this St. Stephen?"

Truit began to sing,

"Good King Wenceslas looked out,
on the Feast of Stephen,
When the snow lay round about,
deep and crisp and even;
Brightly shone the moon that night,
tho' the frost was cruel,
When a poor man came in sight,
gath'ring winter fuel." [12]

---

[12] Opening stanza lyrics to "Good King Wenceslas" Christmas Carol, written by British hymnist John Mason Neale in 1853.

Then he caught his breath and said, "I learned it for the town Christmas Carolin' group a few years back. It was written by an Englishman and has that catchy tune to it. People seemed to be rather fond of it. Anyway, I had to ask, and as it turns out *'on the feast of Stephen'* means the day after Christmas."

"What in the deuce has that to do with anything?" Goff asked.

"I jus' thought it was interestin'," Truitt replied, "with that Dr. Stevens arriving on St. Stephen's day,"

"Y'always was too smart by far," said Goff.

"What ya' mean by that Sheriff?" Truitt said.

"Nothin' boy," Goff said, "Jus' all yer smarts are gonna catch up with ya' someday. People round these parts don't care much fer a know-it-all."

"Okay, Sheriff," Clay got them all back to the main point, "Deekie's got the baby eatin' and sleepin' now, so I think we can hold out till the New Year."

"One more thing, Clay," Sheriff Goff said, "but I'd like to talk in private with ya' on this. So would ya' mind steppin' out on the porch with me?"

"Sure," Clay said, "jus' let me put on my coat."

"Won't take near that long, Clay," the sheriff said, "unless yer more dainty than I think of ya'!"

So Clay and the Sheriff stepped out onto the porch. The air was brisk and Clay was sorry he let Goff talk him out of getting his woolen overcoat. Sheriff Goff reached to the inside of his jacket, fumbling for something that seemed to elude his touch. Goff's face relaxed only after finding it.

"Turns out yer instincts were good, Clay," Goff admitted. "The undertaker went over Miss Margaret's wound real close and damn if he didn't pull this out from the skin under it."

The Sheriff produced a long shard of glass, and dragged Clay over to the window to inspect it in the light. It was a little over an inch long, but very thin. Clay noticed it was not flat at all, but had a slight curvature to it.

"It apparently broke off when Miss Margaret was assaulted," Goff said, "and slid up and under the skin around the main wound. The flesh closed up over it, so the undertaker had a tough time finding it, but given what ya' found on that dead dog's tongue, he kept lookin'."

"Odd thing is," Clay said, "why would there be any glass a't'all on that animal's tongue?"

"I think the glass shattered when Miss Margaret was attacked," Sheriff Goff said, "and the stray came afterwards and found her dead. Likely licked her face clean tryin' to revive her. Remember the lack of blood and how Deekie said her face powder was all smeared, like she had jus' begun takin' it off?"

"Yeah, but..." Clay thought through the facts, "where did the gypsy get the glass to attack the old lady."

"Could be from a knick-knack taken from inside the old woman's house," Goff offered, "as it looks like the gypsy woman and her baby was jus' another pair of stray's Miss Margaret had taken in. Maybe she caught the gypsy stealin' from her. Maybe she was stealin' her fancy glasswares to sell on the streets along with the roses Miss Margaret already allowed her to take from the hot house out back. That's my theory, anyways"

"So ya' think they might have fought in the house?" Clay asked. "But then how'd Miss Margaret get out back across from Schilling's workshed?"

"Remember the tracks in the grass like someone had dragged a body out there?" Goff reminded him.

"But those stopped a few feet away from Miss Margaret's body," Clay thought through it all. "The gypsy woman lifted her up and carried her those last few feet? Besides that, there wasn't no blood in the house, was it?"

"No, we didn't find any," Goff answered. "Still, can't rule that out jus' yet, but I'm with ya'. It looks more like Miss Margaret was attacked outside by the fence, not far from the German's lot line on that creek. Close near to his workshed on the other side."

"And what does this German do in that shed?"

"He's what's called a *Glasbläser.*"

"In English, Sheriff, if ya' please."

"He's a glassblower. Makes baubles and such out of colored glass to sell all over the county. I think the ones Miss Margaret had in her living room came from him directly. They're fancy looking things of all different colors of glass."

"But that bit of glass ya' have there from under Miss Margaret's wound is clear," Clay observed.

"That's about the only thing in this case so far that is," said Sheriff Goff. "And we're on a short fuse before all hell breaks loose and the trial is on us. Think I'll visit that Hun and his workshed soon enough."

Chapter Twelve

Secrets of the Workshed

Sheriff Alpheus T. Goff finally got around to visiting the workshed of Herr Heinrich Schilling the next day. The German protested the unannounced visit, and initially said he could not allow the Sheriff in as he was busy in the process of producing blown glass trinkets for the Christmas Market in the town square.

"Dey have just *runned* out," the German said, "and sold *everythink* I have made. So, I *vork* more. *Schnell, schnell."*

"I can look around while ya' work, Heinrich," Goff said. "Or I can have the judge give y'an order to cease and desist all operations until I get my inspection done. If he does, I might jus' post Deputy Gilmore in yer shed to make sure no work goes on until I git here. And given my busy schedule, that might rightly take a full week or two. Pick yer poison."

"Ahhh!" Schilling spoke in sharp German, *"Das ist mir Wurst."*

"I don't speak German and ya' know it, Heinrich."

"It is just a German saying - *'That is my braut!'* It means *'I don't really care';* so let's go there now."

The German led Sheriff Goff to his workshed. It was a large shed, approaching the size of a small barn. He fished out the key to unlock it. They stepped inside. It was immaculate, appearing to have been recently cleaned out. Certainly there was little evidence of any work in progress.

Sheriff Goff walked over to the main workbench. He looked in several containers filled with colorful powders. "What's all this Heinrich?"

"Deese are the additives used to make color in the glass," he said. "And *deese* are tools I use to form the hot glass." He said holding up blocks and jacks.

Sheriff Goff moseyed over to the furnace and placed his hand just about an inch away from it. "Feels cold, Heinrich. I thought ya' was makin' product in here."

"I *vas* just about ready to begin my *vork,"* he said.

"Looks like ya' jus' got done cleanin' out the place."

"Vhat do you know about glass blowing?" the German asked the lawman.

"Absolutely nuthin,'" Goff admitted.

"Der quality of *der* glass depends on *der* cleanliness of the *ooperation,"* he chastised the sheriff, "so of course, I keep it as *reinigen* as it can be."

"Reinigen?" asked the befuddled sheriff.

"Excuse me, Sheriff," the German said, "it means clean, spotless in English."

"This furnace can get pretty loud in here, can't it?" Goff asked.

"Ya, ya," Schilling said, "very loud."

"But yet ya' heard Miss Margaret scream when the gypsy attacked her?"

"I *vas* cleaning *der* shed *den*," he said, without missing a beat, "so, *ya,* I heard her scream out. *Den I runt* out and *find* her laying on *der grund* with her head *smushed* in. *Der* gypsy *voman* stood over her all bloodied *vith der* rock in her hand. I *tell* you all *dis* already."

"What is this open hole in the wall here for, Herr Schilling?"

"Dat? Dat is for *der blasrohr, der* blowpipe you *vould* say, to rest there. When the glass is hot, very hot, molten you *vould* say, I use *der* blowpipe to breathe *der* air *unto* it, to shape *der* glass or make beads. It is a technique *dat* goes back to the ancient Syrians and Egyptians, and *vas* perfected by *der* Venetians on the island of Murano."

"I thought I saw a pipe comin' out of that hole and runnin' down to the little creek between yer property and Miss Margaret's. Did ya' remove it? I remember the light of yer lamp shone through it like a ball."

"Nein, Sheriff," the German said, "I never had such a pipe as you describe."

"My mistake then," Goff said. "What are these little village wood carvin's over here in this box?"

In a carton were a half dozen village scenes that appeared to be hand-carved. Goff picked one up and sensed that his doing so made the German quite nervous.

"Dose are just *somethink* new I am *speilend vith,"* Schilling said.

"Speilend?"

"Playing vith. Dey are hand-carved in Bavaria. I *tink* I can make *somethink vith* them to sell next year."

"How 'bout these white tiny flakes?" Sheriff Goff asked as he dipped his finger in a container of shredded material not unlike that found by Clay on the surface of the dead dog's tongue.

"Ah, mein Schneewittchen," Schilling replied, instantly interpreting his German for the sheriff, "my Snow Whites. Like the fairy tale*, ya,* with *der* seven dwarves."

"What are these snow white flakes for?" Goff asked.

"My new project, Sheriff," Schilling replied, "but it is *ein Geschäftsgeheimnis,* a trade secret."

"Okay, fair enough. One last question Heinrich," Sheriff Goff reassured him, "has Miss Margaret ever been in here?"

"Here? *Nein, nein.* I treat *dis* like *ein geheimer Ort -* a secret place. No one but you come in here, to protect my secret methods, my artisan *vays.* You understand?"

"I understand fully," Goff said. "It's jus' when we inspected Miss Margaret's body, her one ankles was wet, like she tread in the creek between yer properties. I was jus' wondering if she came over and walked in on ya'."

"Sheriff Goff," the German said, "I protect the secrets of my trade, *ya,* but I *vould* never kill someone who might accidentally *valk* in on me. *Vhat* kind of *Teufel* do you think I am."

"Teufel?" asked Sheriff Goff.

"It means Devil! Monster!" The German shot back.

The sheriff sensed he had touched a nerve. "It's okay, Heinrich, I jus' wondered how her leg went and got so wet if she never came over here by crossin' that creek. That's all."

"I am sorry if I get a little excited, Sheriff," Schilling said. "It is *yust* my German nature. You must understand. After all, your name is German too."

"Alpheus or Goff?" The sheriff asked.

"Alpheus, *nein,* it is from *der* Greek, and means to cleanse. But Goff is German and means *'mist.'* So together your name means to cleanse in *der* mist."

"I'll keep that in mind, Heinrich," Sheriff Goff said. He did not add what he thought, which was, *I'd be in need of a cleansin' mist, all right, iffen I was to cut through the dense smokescreen this glassblower is puttin' up. It's like he ain't wantin' me to understan' 'zactly what the devil goes on in this here workshed.*

Chapter Thirteen

A Mother and Child Reunion

Everything went well throughout the week. The baby was eating and sleeping more regular and along with that came all the mothering that Deekie could provide to Li'l Miss Essie. They had seemed to declare a truce, each on the other. The infant became less antsy, and Deekie found herself loving caring for her.

The sheriff's words from last night seemed to ring over again and again in her ears. Could it be that in as little as a month, Li'l Miss Essie might be hers to keep outright. The thought warmed her, but it still had a tinge of a chill attached in that Deekie did not wish to see anything terrible happen to the child's young gypsy mother.

Still, Truitt had assured her that even if she was found guilty of murdering Miss Margaret, the gypsy mother was all but guaranteed not to hang, with her being a woman and all. The county had had other murderesses who spent the rest of their lives in a ladies' prison. Someone would have to care for this child, for if a jail cell was no place for Li'l Miss Essie, then a prison cell was even worse.

So why shouldn't she and her Virgil raise the little one as their own? Would the judge hold it against them that they were not married? If it took that, Deekie was sure she could talk Clay into getting hitched for the child's sake. Their Li'l Miss Essie was now yawning, in need of a nap.

Deekie and Miss Essie could not sleep up in the loft, because the only way to do so was to pull oneself up a series of planks nailed into the cabin's interior wall, on a sort of makeshift ladder. They had no room to put in stairs. It had never been a problem for young Truitt when he slept there, nor for even Deekie who occupied it now. Clay took a while to get used to climbing those planks with just his one hand, but like everything else in life after the war, he seemed dead set to master it quickly and did so.

There was no way Deekie was going to risk climbing that wall with Li'l Miss Essie. Instead, Clay threw down the tick mattress and they all slept on the cabin floor, as they had done before the cabin's rebuild when Truitt's new room was added.

Deekie would put Li'l Miss Essie down each afternoon for a nap and by doing so finally carved herself out some time to read. Of course, she devoured the book she had borrowed from Miss Margaret's collection, that being *Notre Dame de Paris,* but better known to most as *The Hunchback of Notre Dame.*

In fact, this American edition bore that Hunchback title on its opening interior page, but the blue leather cover with gold lettering simply read *"Notre Dame de Paris, 1833."* Deekie had noticed a set of nine other volumes with matching leather covers, with a gap on the shelf from where this book was taken, so she figured Miss Margaret must have had them rebound in leather as a set. She could only imagine how much that must have cost. She could never think of having so much money to squander on such a frivolous nicety as that book set.

She was fascinated by what she read. Set in Paris of 1484 AD, even then, the cathedral of the title was over 200 years old - older by far than the United States was then.

As for the gypsies, the French believed these beggarly people who roamed the streets of Paris were of Egyptian heritage. She learned in French someone from Egypt is called an "égyptien," which soon was corrupted by the masses to "gypsy." But Miss Margaret had made pencil notes in the margins of some pages, including, *"In reality, the Romani people who were mistaken to be from along the Nile were a wandering nomadic tribe who had actually originated from the Indian subcontinent."*

Deekie did not understand the word *"nomadic,"* but swore to remember it to look up next time she had access to a dictionary. She liked reading, and loved discovering new word meanings. It was like a game to her.

Deekie read about how long ago in the 15th century in Paris the gypsies were severely discriminated against. They were viewed as beggars, thieves and even witches. Deekie could not shake the tale her Virgil had told her of how the German Schilling had repeatedly referred to her as a *Hex* - the German name for a witch. In the margin of that page, Miss Margaret had even penciled in the words, *"Apparently, the bias against these people had not changed much in four hundred years."*

"Virgil," she said, "I need ya' to watch over Miss Essie for a bit."

"Why?" Clay asked. "I got my own chores need tendin' to."

"Well, it's Thursday. I need to get to Sheriff Goff's office and collect my two and a half dollars."

"I figured you'd be takin' Li'l Miss Essie up to see her mother."

"I think it best not to," Deekie said. "Might tear that young women's heart up all the more."

"Naw," Clay corrected her, "what ya' really thinkin' is it's best not to remind her that child is hers, not yours. I seen ya' becomin' more and more attached to that little one. 'Magine how much that mama misses her li'l gal."

"That woman is goin' to be tried fer murder in but a few weeks more…"

"And that is why she needs to see her daughter," Clay said forcibly, "to see that her baby gal is bein' properly tended to and looked after. That poor woman is bein' railroaded. At, least give her the peace of knowin' her daughter is safe and well."

"What if she gets angry at me…" Deekie said.

"I ain't ever known ya' to be afraid of nuthin', Deeks."

"It ain't so much I am scared as…"

"…as guilty," Clay finished her thought.

"Yeah," Deekie said, lowering' her head. "But not for takin' her baby, I done jus' what the sheriff asked…"

Clay finished her trail of logic again. "…But for secretly wishing ya' could keep Li'l Miss Essie forever."

Deekie began to cry and Clay knew he had hit her soft spot. Turned out to be a hard spot to find, let 'lone hit, with her covering it up all these years with her toughness and grit. Still, Clay long knew she had the underpinnings as soft as any woman's. He slid close to her wrapping his arm 'round her.

"Take Li'l Miss Essie wit' ya'," he said. "Bundle her up good and tight. Her mama needs her almost as much as ya' want to keep her. Well, more, I'm sure. Much, much more."

"Yeah," Deekie sniffled, "I'll do jus' that."

Miss Deekie walked the mile in the cold to Sheriff Goff's office only to find his deputy, Howard Gilmore, sitting comfortably behind the lawman's desk. Howard was a short, boyish looking man with a barrel of a belly that seemed to be slung low from his scrawny shoulders. In Sheriff's Goff chair, he looked like some medieval serf caught laying out relaxed at the absent duke's dinner table, Deekie thought.

"Where's Alpheus?" she asked.

"Ya' know he don't like ya' callin' him like that," Howard said.

"Well, iffen he pays me like he said he would today, I'll call him whatever he wants me to."

"Pliss, Pliss," came the gypsy woman's cry from over Howard's shoulder, followed by some unintelligible garble in that dang foreign tongue. The gypsy woman had heard Deekie's voice and even though she could not see the bundle Deekie carried inside her overcoat, she thrust her arms through the cell bars begging for her daughter from whom she had been separated for an entire week. The woman's pleading stabbed away at Deekie's hard outer exterior, her shield against the outer world's judgements.

"Well, ya' best let her hold her chil'," Howard said.

"Jus' as soon as I get paid," Deekie said.

Howard reached into a desk drawer and flipped a brown manilla pay packet at her. It slammed down hard on the wooden surface of the desk.

"Sheriff Goff said to consider yerself paid for the comin' week," Howard said, "and he wants to know if yer having any problems that need to be reported…"

"Pliss, Pliss," came again the plaintiff plea from the gypsy woman, her arms outstretched through the cell's bars as far as they could be. They began to sway, begging more intently for the child to be brought to her.

Deekie felt the seed of remorse spread through her like an all-consuming flame. She let the coins in the packet lie on the desk untouched and wandered slowly back toward the gypsy woman's cell. The look in that mother's eyes was sorry incarnate, but tinged with the hope of soon holding her daughter once more. Deekie undid the buttons of her coat to reveal to the woman that her child had been bundled up tight against the chill of the mid-December air.

Howard rousted out of the comfort of the Sheriff's chair and hunted through the keys hanging from his belt until he found the one for the middle cell. Those lockups on either side remained empty. The deputy opened that center cell door enough for Deekie to pass the still tightly bundled infant to its mother's ravenously hungry arms.

The young gypsy woman drew her daughter into the vacant interior bend of her elbow. It had been a feature of her body denied its natural purpose, so much so, that the joint of her elbow ached with disuse. Filled once more, the crook of her arm balanced the infant's weight perfectly, then cradled it up against her breast. The nook then formed between arm and breast caressed the child in a way so dense with nurturing love that it brought tears to Deekie's eyes as she watched. Deekie had been with this child for a straight week, but had never sensed this level of relaxation in it, the total release of all its stress, as it did now in the reunion of its mother's embrace. The infant was in a state of bliss, reunited with all it had ever known, even long before its birth.

Deekie recalled a line from the book Miss Margaret had taken care to underlined,

"Love is like a tree: it grows by itself, roots itself deeply in our being and continues to flourish over a heart in ruin." [13]

A great guilt overtook Deekie, not because of anything alleged against her by the gypsy, but what she incriminated against herself for the love she had kept from this poor woman, this mother denied.

The gypsy's free hand washed delicately over the cradled child, looking for any presence of injury or malformity, but it was soon satisfied in having neither. Then, the skin of her index finger stroked the soft cheek of the chubby smiling face that it had missed so hauntingly for the past week. Or had it been a month, a year, an eternity?

What happened next shocked Deekie to her core. The woman tore her gaze away for a second from her child and gave Deekie a look that did not kill, as she had feared, but somehow froze her in place. The hand lifted from the child's cheeks rising like a fluttering dove and soon brushed gently against Deekie's face. Then, just as gracefully it swept behind her ear and gently grasped the nape of her neck and so delicately pulled her head forward and down through the still open cell door. Deekie instinctively bowed her head in response as the mother's lips brushed lovingly on her forehead. Deekie felt in the fullness of their press a forgiving gratitude. A wave of absolution washed over her, and in the comfort of its warmth, Deekie again envisioned herself nurturing a child.

---

[13] Victor Hugo, "The Hunchback of Notre Dame," American Edition 1833

"I think she jus' said thank ya' for the way ya' done took care of her chil'," said Howard Gilmore. He had stated the obvious, and it sounded hard and crass compared to the dignity she had felt throughout the moment.

Then the mother turned away with her child, still nooked in place against her torso, to return to the cot that had become the center of her detention. She sat down and poured every ounce of her love over the child as she prepared to feed it.

The fat meaty deputy's hand clutched Deekie's shoulder and pulled her back from the open cell door.

"Best I close this back up," Howard said, "for now. If ya' have some business on the square, go ahead and take care of it. When ya' come back, I'll give ya' the chil' back to take home again."

Deekie could not say anything. She fought the guilt within her as the grace of the mother's love was swept aside by the harsh reality of his words, battered into submission by their coarseness. He had said nothing offensive, but his words were heavy with regret, in contrast to the lightness of the mother's touch given so wholly to her precious baby, and to the woman who looked after her.

Deekie fought the urge to cry, and while Deputy Howard Gilmore locked the mother and child together in that center cell once more, Deekie stormed out of the sheriff's office, altering her direct line to the door only enough to sweep her hand over the desk and retrieve the packet of advance pay for the coming week.

Chapter Fourteen

eekie rushed across the square as if trying to outrun her emotions. Clearly the young gypsy mother had been thankful for the care she had given to the child, but the guilt Deekie felt of secretly wishing to keep the infant bore through her like termites through unpitched timber. How could she have been so thoughtless to keep the child away for an entire week? Would the gypsy mama's sensitivity churn into bile when the baby was kept again from her for another week? Would the woman who had so compassionately forgiven Deekie regress into a grieving wreck after the passing of another seven days without her?

Deekie wrestled with all this grief and remorse as she stormed toward Sayre's Drug Store. She almost had forgotten about the gift for Clay. All she thought about was that mother holding her baby close again, and her having to take it back away again.

Deekie walked right past Mr. Owen's stall of commerce. She seemed to notice some relief in him that she had not stopped. She walked to the pharmacy counter and opened the manilla pay packet and took out the fifty cent piece she owed the druggist. This left two trade dollars inside for her to spend in any way she might find to be appropriate.

"I done told ya' I'd be back today and here I am," Deekie said brashly. "So, here's the fifty cent I owed ya' for the bottle and other things."

The druggist looked down at the coin on the counter, and then laid another just like it next to it. He flat palmed the two and slid them across to Deekie.

"Sheriff Goff stopped in to vouch fer ya', Miss Deekie, and said we was to give ya' whatever ya' needed fer the little one and to bill his office directly for it. Said the bottle and Injun rubber nipple, the diapers and pins were to be included in that. So here is yer fifty cent piece back."

"Well, what ya' know 'bout that!" she said. But the guilt still rode her like a shadow, and she said she wanted to pay for it anyhow.

"Can't take yer money," the druggist said, "done been billed and paid by the sheriff."

"Then give me three cans of that Eagle Brand condensed milk," she said.

"If it's fer the child I'll still have to bill it to Sheriff Goff," he said.

"You'll do no such thing," Deekie burst out upon hearing this. She was determined to turn her blood money into milk money. "It's not fer the child, it's fer Virgil. I assume this stuff is fit to feed grown ups, ain't it? And don't ya' dare bill it to Alpheus. I'll check on it, be sure."

"It certainly is fit fer Mr. Clay. As fer the payment, well, anything you say, Miss Deekie," the druggist replied with a soft smile and a wink. "But don't let the sheriff hear ya' calling him by his Christian name, he don't take to it lightly."

She slid the two half dollar coins back across the counter to him. "That should cover the milk. As fer how I care to address the sheriff, that's my business."

Deekie took up the three cans and shoved them into her pockets. As she did, the druggist slid back a dime piece to her as her change, which Deekie was quick to pick up.

"Wait a minute," the druggist called out. "You seem to be in need of a poke…"

"What?" Deekie said, not understanding his meaning.

"Do ya' want a poke to carry yer cans in?" he said, holding up a paper bag.

"Oh! Yeah, give me that," she said tersely.

"And don't forget to stop at Mr. Owen's stall on the way out," the druggist said. "He too has something for you."

Those words stirred Deekie's memory about the snow globe. This would be the perfect opportunity to carry it home. Even if her Virgil spotted her, she could keep that Christmas gift in the poke, outta sight.

She wandered over to the Owen's commerce stall and said hello to its proprietor, then said she was ready to take her snow globe. Mr. Owen looked pale and concerned as she made her request for her property.

"I'm right sorry to tell you, Miss Deekie, I can't give it to you. I don't have it no more."

"Why ya' dirty rotten scoundrel," she exploded, "ya' done gone and sold it out from under me to some train ridin' high-fallutin' type outta *May-retta* or such."

"No, Miss Deekie, nobody from Marietta nor Atlanta even. I would never dream of selling something that was already paid fer."

"Then jus' where is my snow globe, Mr. Owen?"

"It's just that the man who makes them came and took it back."

"So, Mr. Owen, this man come all the way from Vienna, Austria?"

"Well, I may have stretched the truth a bit. But he did say he learned how to make the snow globes in Vienna. He's a local now. I told him it was already sold, and as such I could not return it to him. He asked just to look at it. When I gave it to him, he turned and walked out without saying a word. I tried to stop him, but with little success. Of course I will reimburse you your two silver trade dollars."

"I don't want my silver back. I want my property." Deekie said. "It was bought and paid fer. Who is it that makes these snow globes round here?"

"I have been requested not to say," the vendor defended himself. "I have my professional reputation to think of. You can threaten me with yer six-shooter all ya' want, but I will never tell."

"Mr. Owen," she began softly, "I would never think of wastin' a bullet over such a triflin' matter as this. And I am glad y'are thinkin' of yer mercantile reputation, because my Virgil's brother is the Clerk of the County Court, and as such knows every sharp-tongued lawyer in this here town. He will lead me to one who has the temperament of a wildebeast and will tear yer reputation up in tatters. Now, that's not a threat, only a peek into your near future lessen ya' tell me who took my snow globe."

Mr. Owen did not take long to weigh his decision. "They are made by the German craftsman, Herr Heinrich Schilling, as are the many other glass baubles in my case. Would you like to peruse some of his other fine works?"

Deekie looked down on the various animal shapes in blue, crimson and various other colors.

"Would you like to peruse some of his other fine works?" she mocked the merchant in a nasal repeating of his words. "No, sir, I would not! I already knew the answer before ya' confirmed it fer me. I will take this up with Mr. Schilling himself. Thank you very much."

With this, Deekie picked up her poke and headed for the door to the square beyond.

"You mean Herr Schilling," Owen said, "that is how he prefers to be addressed. Don't leave yet. Here are your two dollars back."

"Those are yer two trade dollars,[14]" she yelled out without looking back as she reached the door. "That snow globe was bought and paid fer, and as such is my property. That German stole my property, plain and simple, and I intend to git it back."

---

[14] The Coinage Act of 1873 (often referred to as the "Crime of '73") established the US Silver Trade Dollar. They are exceedingly rare today, and those in PROOF condition and bearing the Philadelphia Mint's markings are worth thousands of dollars.

Figure 1: United States Silver Trade Dollars from 1875

Figure 2: First Usage of Borden's Canned Eagle Brand
Sweetened Condensed Milk with Bald Eagle Trademark
featuring Gail Borden's replica signature (1858).

Chapter Fifteen

The Reckoning

Deekie spent as much time as she could that early afternoon moving about the town square. When the bite of the December air proved too harsh to take, she would visit the various shops. If their proprietors gave her the usual hard time, as she was known to look at goods on display but almost never buy anything, she would jingle the two dollars and ten cents in coins she carried. To the local merchants, upon seeing that much money, she would be as welcome as the Commodore Vanderbilt was in the town of Nashville, where the university bearing his name had been founded two years earlier. [15]

As she killed time to give the gypsy woman as many intimate minutes as possible with her baby in that cold jail cell, she kept thinking two separate and very different thoughts.

The first thought she could not escape was of that gypsy woman's kiss of forgiveness on her forehead. She thought it to be the exact opposite of Judas' kiss on the cheek of Our Lord, Jesus. After all, Christ was guilty of nothing, whereas Deekie had secretly hoped for Miss Essie to remain her own, and had driven from her mind the dire consequences that would mean for the jailed mother.

---

[15] The Commodore's familial relation George Washington Vanderbilt II
would not begin construction of the famous Biltmore Mansion and Estate.
in nearby Asheville, North Carolina for another 14 years (1889).

She wished not for the gypsy to be executed for or even imprisoned for her crime, assuming she had even committed it. Yet Deekie was greatly ashamed of her unspeakable desire for something to happen to allow her to retain the child. In contrast to Judas' kiss of condemnation, the woman's kiss was the truest opposite. It was sheer absolution, Deekie thought, her every sin forgiven, offered in exchange only for the love she had shown and would continue to show the captive woman's helpless daughter.

The second thought that refused to leave her was the strange behavior of Herr Schilling. Even before she had the means to buy her Virgil that fancy snow globe, she guessed it had been made by the German's hands. It was too much of a coincidence for a merchant to be selling glass gifts *"All the way from Vienna"* here in town when there was already a Hun glassblower living in the area.

Why would Schilling need to steal back such a fine work made by his own hand? He surely would profit handsomely from its sale? After all, it was the last one available in the area, with not another expected until after the holidays. Why not allow it to be sold?

The answer she kept coming back to was two-fold. First, because perhaps this snow globe was tied to the tiff between Schilling and Miss Margaret. According to Sheriff Goff, the dead woman had accused the German of killing her first stray, and ruining her Christmas Roses. Maybe Schilling did not want anyone connecting the snow globe to their feud. Naturally, she wondered if that feud had somehow led to the woman's death. What better way to wipe that trail clean than by making the last snow globe for sale disappear. Especially when it had been bought by the family of Truitt Clay-Harris, the Clerk of the Court.

Deekie was sure of one thing - that Schilling had stolen her property. She was intent on getting it back. If need be by force, then so it would be. Yet, she could not share any of this with her Virgil. This was the first truly nice Christmas gift she ever had the means to buy him. She would not deny him this, and was determined as all git-out that she would not be denied the joy of the giving it to him. She was ready to take on Herr Schilling on her own.

Deekie strolled down the square until she came to the Park Hotel.[16] This had been the hotel that Sherman had used as his headquarters just before having the city burned then starting his vile march to the sea. Like so many of the townsfolk of Cartersville though, the hotel had been scarred by the Yankee's malice, but managed to survive the war.

She wandered inside the hotel to warm up again. She was just opposite the tracks from Sheriff Goff's office. She would linger as long as they allowed her, then walk over and collect the baby and walk on home. She had spent the better part of a dollar on the Eagle Condensed Milk for the child, but the bulk of the three dollars of blood money still stained her pockets. It might as well have been thirty pieces of silver.

Inside the hotel was a merchant selling locally hand-made quilts. Deekie drifted over to it, and asked the woman tending the store which was the warmest, softest quilt they sold. She was shown a large quilt made from Linsey-Woolsey fabric, died red with sumac, that had stitched upon it the traditional "Sea Waves"or fan pattern. Deekie could feel the heft of it immediately in her hands.

---

[16] The Park Hotel in Cartersville stood where city hall stands today. It indeed dated back to before the War Between the States. It would be renovated as the Braban Hotel in the 1930s by C.L. Bradley and B.J. Bandy. It was bought by the city in 1971 and torn down in 1973.

"It has five stitches per inch, and will last your family for generations," the saleswoman said. [17]

"But is it warm? It don't need to last but for a month or so, but it has to be warm," Deekie said.

"I tell ya' what, Miss Deekie," the saleswoman said, "take off that coat of yours and walk out onto the square with nothin but this quilt draped over your dress. If you're not warm, I'll understand your passin' it by."

Deekie draped herself in the quilt and nothing other than her indoor dress and stepped out onto the north end of the square. She was entirely warm, and decided to purchase the quilt then and there. She walked inside, concluded the transaction, and then carried it across the square.

As she walked into the sheriff's office, Deputy Howard Gilmore was still there. Sheriff Goff remained away on business. Gilmore looked up from what he was attending to and called out, "Welcome back, finally. See ya' couldn't wait to spen' that 'ntar pay packet on the square, Miss Deekie. Treated yerself to a fine quilt, did ya'?"

"Not actually, Howard. This is for the gypsy mama. That jail cell is draftier than a horse barn. I'm gonna give it to her."

"No yer not either," Howard informed her. "That's gotta be inspected fer contraband and such."

"Well, then git to it, Deputy," Deekie said. "That poor woman is all but frozen to the bone in there. Come make sure I ain't slit it open and stuck no chisels inside. Look-ee here, I got my receipt from the shop in the Park Hotel if ya' don't believe I jus' bought the dang thang."

---

[17] Description of Appalachian hand-made quilts sourced from the Berrea College Hutchins Library's Quilts in the Appalachian Artifacts Collections website.

Howard took his time but eventually worked section after section through his hands to assure it was pristine, which, of course, it was. Then he open the cell door. Deekie knew the gypsy woman must have been dreading this moment that overshadowed the joy of being reunited with her daughter, but still gave up her baby without a fuss. Deekie took the child, and with her free hand presented the quilt to the woman. A shocked look overcame the gypsy, as if to say, *Really, for me?*

That look made Deekie realize that all the money made from caring for Li'l Miss Essie would go to either the betterment of the child, or to the comfort of its mother. Not a penny more would be spent on either herself or her Virgil.

On her way out of the office with the baby, she ran her hand over the desk and snatched the that week's copy of the latest Cartersville Express. When Deputy Gilmore objected, she simply told him to take it up with the sheriff, as it was agreed that each week it would constitute a part of her pay along with the two and a half dollars owed.

Figure 3: The Old Park Hotel in Cartersville above (top)
and its reincarnation as the BraBan Hotel in the 1930s.

Chapter Sixteen

Back at her cabin, Deekie made her first attempt to feed Li'l Miss Essie the Eagle Brand canned milk. She had already decided not to share with Virgil that the product had been supplied to Yankee soldiers during the War of the Rebellion. The child took to it quickly, perhaps due to the mixture's sweetness. She had been feeding her mostly goat milk sweetened with corn syrup for the past week, but now Deekie was committed to providing what she thought to be the most healthy food for the child.

After Li'l Miss Essie's feeding, Deekie put her down for a nap. The kiss of the child's gypsy mother on her forehead still haunted her. It didn't matter whether that kiss was given in forgiveness for her taking the child away or in gratitude for caring for the infant while the mother was jailed, it still haunted Deekie.

The thought brought up in her a rise of great guilt. She suffered under the weight of how her innermost hope over the last week had been pinned on just how she might be able to keep Li'l Miss Essie to raise as her own. That would surely mean that the young gypsy woman would have to be found guilty of Miss Margaret's murder.

This was not something Deekie desired, but she knew it was the only way she might have any chance of taking Li'l Miss Essie for her own. Only after that kiss did she see the sinfullness of her desires.

Seeing the poor gypsy woman in that cell made Deekie realize that the love of a true mother for the child she gave birth to could never be equaled. In fact, it was made from a tenderness that Deekie had herself never before felt in life until she saw and felt it firsthand there.

To take her mind off her guilt. Deekie decided to read. She would set aside diving deeper into the Hunchback's and Esmeralda's story in Victor Hugo's novel, instead settling on reading the newest edition of the Cartersville Express she had carried home. It had just come out that morning, and Deekie was curious to see how Miss Margaret's murder was covered.

Strangely enough, the paper did not address the events of the murder at all. *The Express's* front page was covered with stories of the Etowah River, detailing its flow and the landmarks along it's banks as it snaked toward Rome, and a very boring column on the efforts of the Comptroller of the Currency to do something or other. There was even a column on miracle cures for everything from Consumption to *"diseases peculiar to woman."* [18]

Shortly after confirming the story was not buried anywhere else within the remaining pages of the paper, Deekie thought to herself, *What good is a local newspaper if it can't cover the biggest story to affect the town since that damned Yankee Sherman came through burning most everything in sight!*

------

[18] All actual notices published in The Cartersville Express, December 9th, 1875

Her Virgil and his brother Truitt returned home shortly after Miss Essie arose from her nap. As Deekie sat in a chair and cared for the infant, Clay saw the paper on the table and asked Deekie if she might read it to him later.

"Ain't much to read," Deekie explained, "other than Dr. J. S. Pemberton's advertisement for his Globe Flower Syrup to treat The Consumption.[19] Sorry that wasn't around when yer Maw needed it, Virgil."

Clay looked astray at her as she bounced the baby on her lap, then decided not to bite at her bait.

"Probably jus' snake oil, anyhow. What's it say about Miss Margaret's murder?" he asked.

But before Deekie could reply, Truitt loudly snapped the single word, "Nothing!"

"How did ya' know that, Truitt?" Deekie asked. "Did ya' read *The Express* earlier today when ya' shoulda been workin'?"

"No," Truitt explained, "I knew because Judge Ferris called in its editor who was plannin' to run a piece on the front page. The judge explained there was to be an upcomin' jury trial for the gypsy woman, and he did not want the pool of men in the county to be swayed one way or the other by an article, so he demanded it not be published."

"And this editor went along with that?" Clay asked.

"He did when the judge started rattlin' off all the trouble he could make for that new version of the paper."

---

[19] This is indeed the same John Stith Pemberton of Columbus who in the year 1886 came up with the original formula for Coca-Cola. In 1888, dying of stomach cancer at only 57 years old, he and his son sold their last share of that business to businessman Asa Griggs Candler for less than $300 (worth about than $10,000 today.)

"Well, then," Deekie added, "that explains this funny looking notice that's several columns wide with almost no words in it, don't it? They must've pulled that article at the very last minute."

"I reckon so," Truitt said, "as the judge just had him in yesterday afternoon. Only gave them last night to yank it out it and replace it with that…"

Truitt slapped his finger hard on the nearly blank final three columns of the front page. He had seen cotton fields in bloom with less white showing through. In this open expanse were sprinkled only a few sparse words on behalf of the new Express by its publisher, Mr. C. H. C. Willingham, offering a weak (and likely rushed) explanation of the community's need of his new paper.

"That German fella' Schilling is constantly in the judge's chambers pressin' him on expeditin' that trial even more," Truitt explained, "but Judge Ferris has been stubborn as a mule that it stays set for the week between Christmas and New Years so those two professors from Franklin College can get here and tell him as to what the gypsy woman might testify."

"I thought it was jus' the one," Clay said, "that Dr. Stevens, that was comin'?"

"It was to be so," confirmed Truit, "but Dr. Stevens said he would only come if he was joined by another man from the college, a Dr. Lavoisier, a Professor of Chemistry. Turns out Sheriff Goff wanted for him to come along too. Had me book 'em both a room over at the Park Hotel."

"That's only two weeks away," Deekie said. "How on earth are we ever gonna have 'nuff time to prove that poor gypsy woman is innocent?"

Clay's head snapped about sharply upon hearing Deekie say these words. "I'm right proud to hear ya' say that, Deeks. As attached to Li'l Miss Essie as ya' been becomin', I feared ya' might be wantin' to prove she done it. I can't see how possibly how she could have, myself."

"Say more, Virgil," Deekie insisted.

"Well, it don't sound like much," Clay said, "but everybody watchin' her says she's right-handed."

"So?" Then Deekie remembered the gypsy took the baby into the nook of her right arm in the jail cell.

"Well, that night when Schilling held her bloody arm up high, it was her left. Even had that stone covered in Miss Margaret's blood been in her right hand, she couldn't possibly muster up enough force to tear up the old woman's scalp the way it did. Her head wound started on the outside and slanted back to the center. Whoever did this was right-handed all right but real powerful, and they used something more ragged than a small smooth stone.

"Yer right, Virgil, I don't think she murdered Miss Margaret," Deekie replied. "I took her daughter up to her today. Poor thing, doesn't have an ounce of guilt in her. I'm not even sure she understands she's bein' accused of murderin' that ol' woman. She might think she's jus' a witness bein' held fer trial or something. Who can tell what's runnin' through her gypsy mind?"

Deekie did not elaborate on how her own guilt had taken over her thinking. Best that be left unsaid.

"Besides, Virgil," Deekie added, "that German is actin' somethin' a might odd, ain't he?"

"How ya' reckon?" Clay quizzed her.

His question caught her off guard. She didn't want to give away the surprise of her Virgil's Christmas gift, so she couldn't tell him how Herr Schilling had stolen back the snow globe she had already paid for. Her mind raced for an answer that she could share with her man.

"Well," she stammered, "Truitt here keeps sayin' how Schilling wants nuthin' more than to get this thing to trial as fast as he can."

"That's a fact, Clay," Truitt added.

"And had ya' not wandered upon that crowd that night," she went on, "there's no tellin' what he might have roused them folk to do by takin' the law in their own hands. Thank God ya' and Sheriff Goff come along when ya' both did. It coulda got right nasty."

"Yuh," Clay said, "I see yer point."

Deekie sighed to herself, having kept everything else regarding the German a secret.

"Virgil," she said, "I have done some decidin' of my own. I am not goin' to wait another week before I take Li'l Miss Essie back up to her mama. I'm goin' to go let them visit together on both Monday and Thursday."

"Well, that's yer doin'," Clay said, "but that's a lot of walkin'. What will ya' do with yerself while the gypsy woman attends to her chil'?"

"I got a little necessary chore of my own to attend to," she admitted, "but ya' don't need worry yerself none as to what it is."

Chapter Seventeen

The Little Necessary Chore

eekie took the bundled-up Miss Essie on the mile long march to Sheriff Goff's office. She herself wore a thick woolen overcoat, and hidden below it, Deekie carried the Colt Navy Six that Virgil had given her long ago. It was the matching gun to the one her Virgil carried round town. This was the pair that Clay's gunsmith *Diddy* had converted over for him during the war.

The gypsy woman smiled broadly with the unexpected visit of her daughter. She again pulled Deekie's forehead to her lips and kissed it forgivingly, or perhaps thankfully. In either case, the act meant so much to Deekie that she would have been severely depressed if the gypsy woman had not again offered it up.

This time, Sheriff Goff was in the office. Deekie asked him where he had been the Thursday before, and surprisingly, the sheriff shared his whereabouts with her.

"I took the train down to Big Shanty, [20]" Goff said. "Word was they had a caravan of them gypsies 'bout town causin' a stir, so I wen't down to see Sheriff Otho Pierce. Sure enough, they had gypsies come through. He thought they were still be about, but hadn't roundup any jus' yet."

---

[20] The town of Big Shanty, 17 miles south of Cartersville, later changed it's name to Kennesaw Georgia under its 1887 City Charter

"They done anythin' to hurt anyone down there?" Deekie asked.

"Nope," Goff replied, "other than some panhandlin' and such. Sheriff Pierce said he'd let me know if any of them got into any real trouble."

"And ya' think," Deekie asked further, "that these are the group that she belongs with?"

"Sounds likely, don't it," he said, "as we don't git their kind traipsing through these parts very often. I figure if Sheriff Pierce can find one of them that speaks some English, we can have him shipped up here and let us know what she's got to say fer herself."

"And maybe explain to her the trouble she's in…" Deekie added. "But iffen ya' do bring one such gypsy here that speaks their tongue, how ya' reckon to know if he's even tellin' ya' true what she done said? They could be makin' up some grand scheme and ya'd never know, would ya?"

"I guess that's jus' a risk we'll have to take until them college professors git here day after Christmas." Then, Sheriff Goff said somethin' that she did not expect. "If I have to wait until the day before the trial for them professors to come, chances of me figurin' out what really happened are slim to none."

"So, ya' don't figure she killed Miss Margaret?" Deekie said.

"Don't know fer sure," he said, "but I got one German glassblower actin' a might strangely. There's some piece to all this I feel I'm still missing, and not bein' able to talk to that accused gypsy woman ain't helpin' none."

"She didn't kill Miss Margaret," Deekie said. "I can attest to that."

"Based on what, 'zactly?" Goff asked.

"A woman's 'ntwition" Deekie said. "Look how carin' she is with that li'l girl. Like a mama goose and her goslin'."

Goff looked at Deekie strangely. "Ever get too close to a mama goose and her li'l ones. They get a might stirred up. They'll come after ya'. If they was big 'nuff, they'd kill ya', no doubt."

Deekie made her way through the cold morning air back to the scene of the crime. She was careful to come up on Miss Margaret's property, acting as if she was looking for clues on the Taylor-Smith side of the little creek. Yet, her real mission was to get close to and then inside the German's workshed and take back the snow globe she had already paid for. She was sure he would have hidden it in there.

As Deekie walked along the gentle slope of the creek on Miss Margaret's side, she glanced over at the shed for any sign of movement. There was none. After a bit, Deekie stepped over the little creek and made her way up to the shed, but careful to use the structure as cover so she would not be seen from the German's house.

Deekie nearly tripped over a long pipe jutting out of the building through a tight opening. It extended toward the little creek, stopping short, but such that anything draining from the end of the pipe would run down and into its flow.

Deekie followed the length of the pipe, but there was nothing dripping from the opening. She ran her finger over the end of it's opening, where a slow drip fell to the ground. When she put her finger to her mouth she expected to taste some sort of alcohol draining slowly off, but instead Deekie could taste only a strong sweet flavor. In fact, it was overpoweringly sweet.

Deekie then crouched as she walked back up the pipe's length to the window just above the hole in the wall it protruded through. She could not see a thing inside, for the window's glass was frosted. This allowed daylight in for the German to do his work, but kept outsiders from seeing exactly what that work was.

She then slid around the outside corner of the shed, her back up against it as she did, making her feel like some sort of upright serpent. A dog inside the house barked at her movement, distracting her until she realized it could not get out and come after her. Deekie soon found the latch on the shed's door and was surprised it's hasp was not locked.

She stood frozen, recalling words Miss Margaret had underlined from the Hunchback book warning,

"The owl goes not into the nest of the lark." [21]

Well, this is no lark, she thought, *so here goes,* and grasped the door in her shaking hand. Deekie opened it slowly, peered inside, and upon seeing no one, she slithered inside. What she saw there amazed her. There were several large glass vessels, most filled with a clear waterlike liquid. Beneath these glass jars - that was it - they looked like giant rounded jars - beneath them was a drain pan, and its lowest corner funneled into the pipe going through the wall.

---

[21] Victor Hugo, "The Hunchback of Notre Dame," American Edition 1833.

Deekie first would have sworn this was some sort of moonshining operation, but the overpowering sweet taste that still lingered in her mouth told her it must be something else. There was no smell of alcohol either, even inside the confines of the shed.

Deekie raised her eyes to spot several snow globes sitting on the work bench. They all looked similar in appearance, but each hand-carved village scene inside them was slightly different. Then she saw it. Her snow globe.

Deekie knew it was hers because the third roof in the little alpine village had that oddly shaped chip missing from its corner, just as she had observed in the drug store. She picked it up and turned to make for the door, when a large figure stood blocking its opening. In his hands, the man held a long iron rod.

"Miss Deekie," Schilling said to her, *"Yust vhere* do you *tink* you are *goink* with my *Schneekugel?"*

Deekie slipped the object into her woolen coat's large pocket, her hand shaking even more at having been caught, making her fear she might drop her Virgil's gift. Still, that was where her concern ended. She knew this was her snow globe, bought and paid for. She intended not to turn it over to the man who had stolen it. Not even if indeed he was the man who had made it in the first place.

"If that last word means snow globe…" she began.

"Ya, ya, it does…" he confirmed.

"…then y'are greatly mistaken. This one snow globe I purchased from John T. Owen inside Sayre's Drug Store down on Main Street. Paid in full with legal tender. He told me ya' stole it back."

"Vhat? Stehlen? How could I steal *vhat* I make *vith* my own hands? No, dere is no *stehlen,* I *yust* bring your *schneekugel* back here to fix it. It has minor defect *dat* I *vant* to make perfect, *dat* is all. So take it from your coat pocket and return it to the *vorkbench. Ya?* I *vill* return it to you as soon as I *revork* the item and bring it to your home, y*a?"* the German said warmly.

"If yer taking 'bout the chip in the roof of the village house, I don't mind it stayin' that way. I come to like it. That way I reckon I will always know it's mine."

"Der Dorfhausdach? Nein! Das problem is not the roof of the village house" *he said.* "It is *somethink else, so please* return it to the *vorkbench, ya?"*

"Return it to the *vorkbench?"* Deekie repeated, complete with her mockery of his accent as she moved her hand inside her coat. "Naw, I don't reckon I'll be doing' that anytime soon."

The German took a step closer to intimidate her. He pounded the iron rod into the palm of his left hand in a threatening manner.

"Return it to *der vorkbench!* If you do not, then I cannot permit you to leave here *vith* it, Miss Deekie. It is *verboten* for you to leave *vit der schneekugel* as it is. So, I repeat, return it to the *vorkbench, ya?"*

"Herr Schillink," she said, still mocking his accent, "ya' might have well scared off other women with yer flusterin' ways, but I ain't like other women. And I ain't alone, either. Fact is, I brought along six of my friends."

"Nein," Schilling said, "I *vatched* you as you *valked* up *der* side of Miss Margaret's property. You are alone."

Deekie slowly produced the Colt Navy Six from under her coat and pointed it dead center at his abdomen. The German stared at it, but refused to move away from her.

"You *vill* not *schoot dat* at me," he said cooly.

Deekie pulled back the hammer with her thumb. "I will iffen ya' make me. Now move aside, *Herr Schillink.*"

Heinrich Schilling glared at her but did not budge until she moved her aim from the center of his protruding belly to just below it. Only then did he truly appreciate the gravity of his personal risk and slowly stepped to one side.

"Now," she said, "I know yer fixin' to drop that iron rod to the ground so's I can squeeze past ya'"

The German did so. Deekie made a shallow circle around him, keeping the gun leveled as it was before, always between them. When she reached the door, she had one last thing to say.

"Don't come to our spread looking fer this, either. Anybody nosin' round our property gets shot at first, and 'dentified later. Sheriff Goff says that's a perfectly lawful way of conductin' ourselves. So, good day, *Herr Schillink.*"

The German was fuming, and the only words to escape from him as she left were in his native tongue. He muttered, *"Auf Wiedersehen, Hündin."*

Chapter Eighteen

The Allegation

Two days later, Sheriff Goff rode his horse onto their property. Deekie walked out to call to him as he rode up the path, yelling out that her Virgil was not there. He had found himself some day work and would not be home until sunset.

"Actually, Miss Deekie," the sheriff said, "I have come to talk to yerself, not Clay."

"Is it about the baby?" she asked. "Did ya' come to take Miss Essie back?"

"What in the deuce? No," he said. "I come with an order from Judge Ferris to take that Navy Six revolving pistol away from ya'."

"Why?" she protested. "I got every right to protect myself. What's this all about?"

Sheriff Goff dismounted from his bay mare and tied the horse off to a porch post. "Herr Schilling went to see the judge complaining ya' leveled yer Navy Six at him, and stole one of his snow globes."

"I did no such thing," she said. "Well, I sure didn't steal from him. I bought that snow globe as a Christmas gift for Virgil. Got a receipt inside, and ya' can check with Mr. John T. Owen himself down at Sayre's."

"I already did," Goff confessed. "So I won't ask fer the snow globe even though the judge instructed me to. No, that is yers to keep, I reckon, but, ya' did level yer Navy Six at him then?"

"Sure I did," she admitted, "but only because he was threatenin' me with a piece of metal and blockin' my way from gettin' outta his shed."

"So, it's true," the sheriff asked, "that ya' broke into his workshed? Now be careful how ya' answer this, cause if ya' say ya' were, then I am told to bring ya' in to be charged with trespassin'."

Deekie took his warning to heart and decided to lie. She knew the sheriff would accept it at face value because if she was to be arrested, then it meant she could no longer look after Miss Essie. And for sure, the sheriff did not want a crying infant disturbing the peace in his office.

"No, he invited me in to see the many snow globes he had in there," she lied, "that he had brought back in to fix somethin' or other in 'em. I saw mine and took it back and that's when the trouble started. Yeah, I pointed my pistol at him, but only in defense of myself. I feared he gettin' ready to thrash me with that rod he was holdin'."

Sheriff Goff seemed to roll the explanation around in his mind for a moment or two. Then he said simply, "Okay, Deekie, I'll accept that fer now, but ya' still gotta give me that Navy Six. Judge's orders. Ya' can petition him fer it tomorrow if ya' like, but he's got Herr Schilling wedged so far up his hind quarters that the Kraut can count the gaps of sunlight comin' through the judge's teeth. I recommend ya' give me the gun and let things lie until the dawn of the New Year at least."

"Oh, dang it, Sheriff," Deekie said, as she stormed into the cabin. "Jus' wait here a minute."

Deekie came out with the weapon, holding it by the barrel and surrendered it to Sheriff Goff.

"That's a easy way to shoot yerself," Goff said, noting that in handing the gun to him she had pointed the barrel right at her own chest.

"It ain't loaded," she said thrusting the revolver at him. "I'm not thick! I done took the bullets out of it."

"And where are they?" Sheriff Goff asked.

"Why?" She snipped at him. "Did Judge Ferris ask fer them back too?"

"No, I reckon he didn't," Goff confessed. "Just' ordered me to confiscate yer gun."

"Ya' know," she said, "Virgil's got the matchin' pistol from the pair, but he ain't here jus' now."

Sheriff Goff winked at her. "Judge said just to git yer gun, Deekie. Said nothin' bout Clay's. At least yer man can put them bullets ya' took out to some good use, should he need to. I'll see ya' tomorrow when ya' come up for yer pay and the next edition of *The Express.*"

After which, Sheriff Goff saddled up and rode off.

When Clay came home that evening, Deekie was still riled up over all that had come to pass. She told him about the sheriff's visit as she served him up some Brunswick Stew for dinner, with a few lies peppered in for flavor.

"Alpheus said several townswomen spoke to Judge Ferris complainin' on about my carryin' that Navy Six all over town. One even made up a tall tale that I pointed it at her. The sheriff wouldn't dare tell me who it was though. So I had to turn it over."

"But ya' didn't point it at her, did ya'?"

"What, point a pistol at a lady?" Deekie protested. "No, Virgil, I did no such thang."

"Well, Deeks," he said, "I'd offer ya' mine, but knowin' ya' as I do, I suspect it would only soon 'nuff be taken from y'also."

"I know that person is gonna come here looking fer my ..." Deekie started to say, only then realizing she nearly gave away fact that she had bought a gift for him. She had thought earlier to leave all that out of the conversation, but now she had gotten sloppy and nearly slipped up.

"Come here? Lookin' fer what?" Clay asked.

"Aw, Virgil, nothing in *perticlar*... jus' looking fer any excuse to harass me further. That's all."

Deekie caught herself just in time. She was sure by then that the German had smashed the old woman's head in with a snow globe. It had to be why he was taking all the others from the people who had bought them to be fixed in his workshed, as if to wipe away some connection to himself through these things. Despite all this, Deekie knew she couldn't mention the snow globe or Schilling to Clay.

"Y'alright, Deeks?" her Virgil asked.

"I dunno, Virgil," she balked, "I'm jus' a bit rattled by all this, I reckon. Hey, whatever came of that piece of glass they took from Miss Margaret's head wound?"

She figured it to be a good time to change subjects.

"That's odd. What's got y'askin' about that?" Clay was surprised by her question.

"Well, I was wonderin' if it tied that Schilling fella to the crime. That was what ya' was thinking, wasn't it?"

"Yeah, but that piece of glass they took outta Miss Margaret had no color a't'all to it," he argued. "Herr Schilling's glass baubles all are colored right nicely."

Not the glass of his snow globes, Deekie thought. *And that would explain the white snowflakes on the dead dog's tongue.* But of course, she could not mention either.

"It's still a mystery," Clay said, "jus' like how that dead stray dog got put atop Miss Margaret's dead body."

Deekie had no explanation for that other than the dog might have bitten the German, who then killed it. But then again, there were no wounds found on the dog at all.

About then Truitt came home and she knew they would all rehash the same conversation again. Before they did, Deekie pulled him aside and told him under no circumstances was he to mention the snow globe or the fact of her being caught in the German's shed. Truitt already knew of it from the judge's order. He agreed he would not mention any of that to his brother.

Later that evening, after Miss Essie had been put down to sleep, Deekie took to reading the Hunchback novel some more. She got to the part of the story where the hunchback Quasimodo was put in the stocks at the Square of Miracles in Paris. He thirsted for a drink of soothing water, but the people only spit on and taunted him. Then, in an act of kindness, Esmeralda, the lovely gypsy girl, gave a drink of water to the disfigured and humiliated character.

Deekie thought of the jailed gypsy mother as Esmeralda. Earlier in the book, when this character was introduced, Miss Margaret had penciled in the margin, *"La Esmeralda means 'The Emerald'."* The nearby text said that that the beautiful dark gypsy girl wore a piece of green glass around her neck for good fortune. It was called "an amulet," another word she could not wait to look up.

Deekie had never heard of someone marking up a book, and thought it must be what rich folk do. It felt funny reading the notes of a dead woman. It was kind of like Miss Margaret was talking to her from beyond the grave.

She thought of the jailed gypsy woman as Esmeralda? She certainly was beautiful enough. In the morning, Deekie would take her child back to her for the second time that week. Would she once more kiss her forehead in gratitude and absolution? Was that the proverbial drink of refreshing water? Did that make Deekie the disfigured one in this story?

Chapter Nineteen

The next day was Thursday the sixteenth. Deekie took Li'l Miss Essie up to Sheriff Goff's office with her. Upon arriving there, the same sequence of events came to pass. The gypsy mother took her child, pored herself over it to assure her daughter was healthy, and then pulled Deekie close to thank her with a sincere and thankful kiss on her forehead. She had the same flash vision of herself nursing a child, but Deekie questioned whether it was another vision or merely a memory from her last visit.

Then the mother took to feeding the infant at her bosom, and Deekie settled in for a long discussion with Sheriff Goff.

"Here's yer twenty bits fer the comin' week," Goff said, handing her the manilla packet holding two trade dollars and a half dollar coin. "I reckon it is well worth the peace of keepin' this office free of that cryin' chil'."

"She's not so bad," Deekie said, "once we come to terms with each other. But she sure perks up when she's with her mama, that's fer sure."

"Deekie," Sheriff Goff said, "I got something I wanted to ask ya' yesterday, but ya' was so riled up I decided to pass on it."

"What was that, Sheriff?"

"I wanted to ask ya' exactly what ya' saw when ya' went into Herr Schilling's workshed."

Deekie explained the big jars of clear fluid and the drain pan. She mentioned the pipe going throught the wall and down to the little creek that she near tripped over. And of course all the snow globes lined up to be reworked.

"I found out he was goin' to everyone Owen sold them things to and asking fer 'em to be returned to him to be reworked," Sheriff Goff said, "but reworked for what?"

"Schilling wouldn't say, other than it wasn't for any nicks in the wooden village pieces," Deekie explained. "All them globes appeared to look jus' fine to me. Didn't ya' see any of that when ya' went there?"

"Naw," he answered, "the German had cleaned up the place. I noticed the hole in the wall and Schilling lied to me about it, too. Said that it was to hold a tool of some sort. None of them big jars was there when I went, neither. No liquids of any kind. I knew he was outright lying to me."

"So, jus' go again and see fer yerself," Deekie said.

"I can't," he said. "Schilling has gone to Judge Ferris and complained about my visit as I had no writ from the court to do so. Now Judge Ferris is restrictin' me from returning until the trial is over. He doesn't want Schilling making yet another fuss. I sure would like to know what is in them big jars of liquid. I wonder if he's runnin' some kinda still in there makin' moonshine."

"I don't reckon so," Deekie said. "First of all, there was no heat, no fire under any of them liquids. Secondly, the few drops I tasted didn't taste of liquor. Naw, it was super sweet, far sweeter than any honey I ever had."

"Then why would he be takin' them snow globes back there? None of this makes any sense," Goff said.

"I got an idea," Deekie said.

"Which is what, 'zactly?"

"I think Herr Heinrich Schilling got into an argument with Miss Margaret that night and he smashed her head in with one of them snow globes. That would explain both the hunk of glass under her scalp and the dead dog having licked up them little snowflakes on its tongue."

"I had the same thoughts," Goff said, "but then again I can't explain how that dog died or even got put there, especially since Schilling was down on the Cassville Road with that crowd when Clay came across them all. That dog's body was still a little warm when I felt at it that night. It surely musta died while we was all on that corner with that rowdy crowd."

"I think she," Deekie flashed her thumb back at the jailed gypsy mother, "came along and Schilling figured since she couldn't talk to no one, he'd blame everything on her. Kinda makes her the perfect patsy."

"I guess we'll find out her story once the professor from Franklin College gits here the day after Christmas."

"Ya' mean Dr. Stevens on the feast of Stephen?" Deekie laughed.

"Jus' so," Goff smiled at her. "Gettin' back to that liquid though, I can't figure what it might be."

"Natural thinkin' says it is whatever is inside them snow globes. Right? Ya' ever seen one them shooken up right good?"

Goff smiled again at Deekie. "Yeah, them flakes seem to hang in the air like snow that jus' don't seem to want to settle out. I find it unusual how Schilling has gone around town collectin' up every one of them that's been sold so far. Like he's gathering up all the evidence against him to hold on to until after the trial."

"That is all except fer the one I bought fer Virgil," Deekie added.

"Ya' best be careful, young lady," Sheriff Goff said. "If yer theory is correct about Schilling usin' a snow globe to kill Miss Margaret, then that man has a lot at risk. And those people at risk start takin' bigger risks of their own. He might do anything jus' to git that last snow globe back."

"Then give me back my Colt Navy Six," Deekie suggested.

"If I could, I would," Goff admitted, "and don't go takin' Clay's gun neither. Judge Ferris is already hotter than a dry creek bed in July."

"Okay, then. Can I stick my nose in that copy of *The Express?*" Deekie asked.

"Sure," Sheriff Goff said, "It's yers, remember? Part of our deal - yer negotiated pay."

Deekie left Li'l Miss Essie with her mother at Sheriff Goff's office, and said she'd return in several hours. She traipsed her way back to their homestead where she invested some more of her time in the book.

Deekie read up to the point where the beautiful Esmeralda, who she envisioned as that jailed young gypsy mother, was being accused of witchcraft by the powerful elites of Paris. They seeded the accusatory thoughts in the minds of the everyday people of that city, who turned strongly against the young gypsy, leaving Esmeralda's only way to stay safe was to take up living inside the Notre Dame Cathedral alongside the disfigured Quasimodo.

Miss Margaret underlined another passage that caught Deekie's attention about Quasimodo, the hunchback. It read,

"The saints were his friends, and blessed him; the monsters were his friends, and guarded him." [22]

Oddly, this quote reminded her of her Virgil, especially when he first got back from the war. All the strange looks his deformity would draw! The saints surely had blessed him by sparing his life, and Willet Blackwell turned out to be one of the very monsters he counted among his friends. Those friends had indeed guarded Virgil from the Union troops the night the town was burned, but reverted to being the very monsters that her man had to destroy in order to save her.

That had been a dark time that she would rather forget, yet it was strange how the notes in this book from a dead woman's pencil brought it all back to life.

─────────────────────────

[22] Victor Hugo, "The Hunchback of Notre Dame," American Edition 1833.

Hugo's hunchback would taunt the crowds outside the cathedral, who were crying for Esmeralda to be turned over to them. He would scream the word *"Sanctuary!"* over and over again from its upper heights amidst the downcast stares of his only real companions, the church's stone gargoyles.

In those times, the word *"Sanctuary!"* had a most definite meaning. Anyone taking refuge in a house of God was granted safety from those pursuing them. The chased were comforted within its walls until a formal judgement was made against them by the courts.

Deekie thought this was exactly what had occurred in the case of the young gypsy mother. No, she was not safely locked away in a house of God, but had her Virgil and then Sheriff Goff not come along when they did, there was no telling what she might have suffered at the hands of that crowd. Now, the jail cell was her Notre Dame, her sanctuary, all the protection she would need until the courts could determine her fate.

Chapter Twenty

The Week before Christmas

On Monday, the twentieth of December, Deekie again trekked the mile up to Sheriff Goff's office to reunite Li'l Miss Essie with her mother. Sheriff Goff was in an excited state when she arrived, for he had just read a telegram from Sheriff Otho Pierce of the town of Big Shanty, near twenty miles in, close toward Marietta.

"Says here," Goff explained, "that they got one of them gypsy men who been roamin' round their town jailed up for vagrancy. Good news is that the man speaks fair to middlin' English. The sheriff offers to bring him here, but can't until Friday since he has a court case he needs to attend to down there."

"Then how can he be sure to make it up here on Friday?" Deekie asked. "What iffen that case ain't over by then?"

"Deekie," Goff said, "Friday is Christmas Eve! No court in the state would hold proceedings on Christmas Eve, now would they? But if he catches the early train we can have our business wrapped up by a respectable hour. And the sheriff is a widower, so he'll stay over with the gypsy under his charge until them two professors from Franklin College get here on Sunday."

"Well, he can stay jus' across the square from yer office then," she said, "over at the Park Hotel. Ain't that handy…"

"Nothin' doin'," said Goff. "He'll stay as my and Myrtle's guest at our home. Least we can do fer another lawman assistin' us."

"Well, I'm sure y'ain't likely to have that gypsy fella do the same."

"No, Deekie, he'll be right comfortable in one of these empty two cells." Sheriff Goff swung his head back toward the gypsy mother nursing her child behind him.

Deekie gave her a look, and then peered back at the sheriff. "And yer not worried about them cookin' up some grand story over Christmas Day while y'all revel in plum puddin' and such at the Goff household?"

"No," Goff said, "cause we'll take her statement jus' as soon as the sheriff and his gypsy fella get off at the depot on the 8:42 train on Friday mornin'."

Deekie thought through that logic, and then offered up a question. "Does the sheriff from Big Shanty speak gypsy? Cause iffen he don't, how can ya' be sure what his gypsy fella' is tellin' ya' is 'zactly what she's sayin' to him in that tongue?"

Sheriff Goff was getting a bit tired of all her questions. "It's simple, Deekie. When the Franklin College professor gits here on Sunday, he'll confirm her story fer us. If it don't match up with what this gypsy fella tells us, then we will ask Judge Ferris to delay the trial until we git to the bottom of all this."

"What if she done it, Sheriff? Then what happens?"

"Then she'll go to jail for the rest of her life, I 'magine. That's up to the judge."

"Judge Ferris won't have her hung, will he?"

"I reckon not. They don't hang women, not even women murderers." Goff looked at Deekie like she was thick.

"But they hung that Mary Surratt at the end of the war and she didn't kill no one."

"Come on, Deekie. She was involved in plannin' the plot to kill President Lincoln. She was the only woman ever hung by the Federal Government up until then. This ain't that! No, I figure this gypsy gal won't git the noose."

"Even so," Deekie thought aloud, "what will happen to Li'l Miss Essie?"

"That is also for Judge Ferris to decide. Maybe they'll send her back to that pack of wanderin' gypsies down there in Big Shanty. Who knows? Now, if ya' can stop with all yer questions and leave me mind to my business. We got a real cold snap comin' in and I got a lot to do to prepare for that. S'pose to get below freezin' and stay there the next few days."

"Alrighty then," Deekie said, "I'll be back late in the day to take the girl home with me."

"I advise ya' to stay away from the courthouse, even if ya' got business with Truitt," Goff said. "Judge Ferris was none too happy with ya' pointin' that pistol at the German last week. He would have had me take ya' in jail too were it not fer yer watchin' over that gypsy babe, and I had to fight to convince him of that. I don't need no more ill stirrin's from Judge Ferris, y'understand?"

"Sure I understand," Deekie said. "Yer jus' afeared of Judge Ferris, Sheriff."

When Deekie arrived back at her spread along Pettit's Creek, what she found shocked her. The door to their cabin was wide open, although she was sure she had closed it. When she left, Truitt had already left for the courthouse, and Virgil had gone off in search of day work. It was not like him to return until sunset, even if he was unsuccessful. He would just keep roaming about town looking for some odd chores he could do to earn some pay.

Deekie walked slowly up to the porch and peered into the cabin. It looked like a pack of coyotes or racoons had ripped up the place looking for something to eat. Papers were strewn everywhere. All the drawers of the cabinets were left hangin' open. The garbage pale was overturned and it's filth was spilled out over the floor.

Yet, amidst all this chaos, the pecan pie she had made the night before sat untouched on the counter. Not so much as an edge of the crust was broken away. No, no 'coons or coyotes would have missed this. Someone had waited for her to leave and then ransacked the place. Deekie knew just what that person was looking for.

She grabbed the sharpest knife she had and walked out the front door at a clipped pace toward the bank of pines just before the creek. She looked over her shoulder to make sure no one was following her. She moved between the trees until she found the one into which she had carved a V shaped notch about a foot off the ground.

She used the length of the knife to measure out the distance from the notch. Then she scraped away the pine straw with the knife's blade, revealing the hole she had dug out last week. In it sat the snow globe, just as she had left it, hidden well out of the sight of Virgil.

She picked it up out of the recess of roots and spun it round in her palms. It looked undisturbed. She released a sigh of relief. That damn German, Schilling, had turned her place upside down looking for it. *Why? Why was he so dead set on gettin' hold of it?* she wondered.

Deekie shook the glass ball. Inside it, the frenzy of a blizzard erupted, and the white flakes stayed buoyantly suspended for what seemed a disproportionate time. Yet, they were so peaceful to watch as they floated, too slowly, coming to settle out on the roofs of the hand-carved village inside the globe.

Virgil will jus' love this Christmas present, she thought. She replaced it among the tree's tangle of roots and then covered it over as it had been. Then she trudged back to the cabin and began to straighten up all the disorder left behind by Heinrich Schilling.

Chapter Twenty-one

The Haunting Premonition

Tuesday and Wednesday were uneventful, other than Clay refused to let Deekie out of his sight after hearing her story. Of course, she had to act like she had no idea who the intruder was or what they sought after. Clay stayed closeby, his Colt Navy Six strapped to his right leg. If whoever had the nerve to come after his Deekie returned, he'd be there waiting for them.

Deekie was impressed by her man's dedication to her, but knowing Virgil, she expected nothing less. It was nice to have him close by, as the German Schilling certainly knew by then that she had been disarmed by Judge Ferris. She doubted he'd return with Virgil staying close by. Yet, she still wondered why the German was so determined to get his hands on that snow globe.

Thursday morning came and it was once more time to take Li'l Miss Essie into town to spend some time with her mother. Clay walked with them both along the Mission Trail to Market Street and then on to the town square. On Market Street, across from the Gilreath cottage where Clay had once worked the lawn, they passed by the doors of the Cartersville Baptist Church.

"Virgil," Deekie broke the silence as they walked, "have ya' heard how that Lottie Moon has been doin' over in China over the past two years? I think that is so wonderful fer her to be doin' God's work in that way."

"That's a long way to go to find non-believers," Clay answered. "Lord knows we got plenty 'nuff here in our own country. If men acted as they should in the name of the Lord we'd have had no War of the Rebellion in this country, and I'd still have two full arms to wrap around ya', girl. This country is full of men who claim with their words to love God, but their hearts love war and death so much more. At least the town folks have rebuilt the inside of this church after them damned Yankees tore it down so angrily during the war. Ransacking a place of God, can ya' 'magine? Them men had hearts of stone."

"I was jus' sayin', Virgil," Deekie answered in a frustrated tone, "how much I 'preciate Lottie Moon spreadin' the word of God all the way over in China and ya' gotta go off on another of yer tirades about the war. I know it changed ya', Virgil, but shed yerself of it, already."

"It didn't jus' change me," Clay answered, "it changed us all, it changed everything. And them damn radical Republicans takin' over Congress and now with President Grant in the White House. After what they done to President Johnson, impeachin' him and all, we may never see another Southern Democrat in the White House."

"Like I said, Virgil," Deekie cut him off, by then sorry for ever having broken the cold hard silence of their walk, "ya' need to shed yerself of all that anger. We got it good now. A roof over our heads, food in our bellies, and yer brother Truitt havin' himself a steady payin' job at the courthouse. Be thankful. Things could be worse."

"Could be better, too," he said, after which the silence descended once more between them.

Deekie had never been able to guess what might set her man off about the war. Sometimes, like today, it was the littlest, seemingly unrelated thing. It would bring a darkness over the man who otherwise was as peaceful and kind as you could want a fellow to be. Deekie decided to let the silence settle out between them slowly again like a blanket of snow in that toy globe. After all, they were almost to the town square.

Deekie and Clay entered Sheriff Goff's office around seven-thirty in the morning. Today was the big day, because in just over an hour, the morning train would come into the depot. On it would be Sheriff Pierce of Big Shanty with his English speaking gypsy in tow. Everyone was excited to hear just what the gypsy woman would have to say about what happened on the night of the murder.

"Sheriff," Deekie cried out as they entered the office, "be warned I brought along my Navy Six totin' bodyguard."

"How are ya', Clay?" Goff called out as Deekie swept past him to the woman in the center cell.

"Come on now, Sheriff, open up this cell so this mama can hold her little baby girl."

"Hold yer horses, Deekie," the sheriff said, as he slammed papers in a file which were then flung angrily into the drawer of his desk. "I'm not as spry as I once was."

The sheriff opened the door of the cell and even before the young gypsy mother took hold of her child, the captive's hands reached to gently cradle her visitor's cheeks. She then most delicately stretched upward on her toes to kiss the skin of Deekie's forehead once more.

Just as before, Deekie felt a bolt of emotion surge through her, this time while she still held Li'l Miss Essie in her own arms. For a split-second, as if from within a darkness suddenly illuminated by a flash of lightning, she seemed to be pinned to the ceiling, looking down upon herself holding that child. Or was it another child? She could not tell. In this spectral glimpse, she saw only the outlines of herself and the babe, but bathed in a flash that bleached them in a dazzling pure white. No others within it were revealed; all else was lost in its overpowering brightness. Just the loving image of Deekie holding a child.

When the gypsy reached to take the infant from her, Deekie felt the energy shift to the bond between them, as if a long denied spirit joyously passed from mother to child and back again. Deekie felt them being stitched together by it, merging the separated souls into a single precious unity.

"Well, Deekie," Sheriff Goff said, somewhat startling her back from her incredible second sight, "ya' goin' to let that babe go so her mother can have some time alone with her or not?"

Deekie cast off her split-second reverie, and then handed the infant over to her mother. The love between them quite visibly unfurled like the tenderness of a rose in bloom, so soft and delicately fragrant. As much as she had come to care for Li'l Miss Essie, Deekie knew in that moment she could never possess the same level of care, of affection, of love for that child as its natural mother.

The gypsy sat on the cot and wrapped herself and the baby in the warmth of the gift of Deekie's quilt. Deekie hoped one day she might live to feel that same sacred bond that then so tenderly connected this mother and child again.

"Ya' feelin' okay, Deeks?" Clay asked as she backed away from the cell door as the sheriff closed and locked mother and child in once more. "Yer lookin' a li'l peaked."

"It's nothin' more than a spot chill, Virgil," she said, feeling an emptiness consume her as the vision drained away, leaving a void she might never be able to fill in her life. Perhaps, the gypsy mother taunted her in this way by placing the image of all she truly desired in her mind, if only to haunt her for the rest of her life.

"Deekie," Sheriff Goff said, "I got yer pay packet up here on the desk along with the latest issue of the Cartersville Express. I'm hopin' once the sheriff from Big Shanty and his gypsy arrive, ya' can take the babe overnight while we take the woman's statement. Of course, it might be the last we'll need of yer services. After all, them professors from Franklin College will arrive the day after Christmas, and we might be able to wrap all this up."

"Saint Stephen's Day," Deekie muttered, a sadness having by then so perversely penetrating her being that the stoning of Saint Steven, the first Christian martyr, seemed as if it might be a bearable escape for her.

She walked to the sheriff's desk and picked up the manilla pay envelope and the newspaper. She stepped out into the cold as tears formed in her eyes, unusual for Deekie. The fear of her forthcoming separation from Li'l Miss Essie stirred up a torrent of devastation within her. She had been given a taste of a sacred fruit, only to be denied its sweetness for the rest of her life.

Her eyes were drawn to the Western and Atlantic depot's timetable printed on the front page. The train would arrive from Big Shanty at 8:42 AM, in less than a hour. She feared this would mark the beginning of the end of her time with Li'l Miss Essie. No, she could never care for the child as tenderly or love her as completely, as thoroughly, as her own mother, that much had been revealed to her. But Deekie had grown attached to the child, admittedly if only to fill the vacant moments of her own life.

She knew one of several fates would await the child. If the gypsy mother was found innocent of all charges, as Deekie truly hoped, the child would return with her to their wandering life. But if the woman was found guilty, and this was looking to be more probable, or so Deekie thought, then the child would either be returned to its people by the Big Shanty gypsy translator, or would be permanently placed in another home in town.

Deekie knew that home would never be with her and her Virgil. They lived together in sin, unmarried, out on the edge of town. They were tolerated by the townspeople because of her Virgil's war record, but no esteem more than toleration was lasting. Sure, the townsfolk all hooted and hollered on his return from the war, and after the shootout on Three Sisters Mountain, and even in their homecoming as heroes from Texas, but all that seemed to last only as long as a morning frost on a Southern spring day. After it all evaporated away, they were allowed to amble about town, gathering the sidecast glances of the townswomen and the insincerely cold courtesy offered by their husbands. No, Li'l Miss Essie would be placed with one of the prim and proper families in town. One that could provide for her, and scrub away the traces of her wandering heritage.

Deekie tried to lose herself in reading the front page of The Express, noting article titles on the disastrous conditions of the local roads and how they hampered commerce; on the pending visit to Atlanta of the Ohio Statesman George H. Pendleton; and a reprint of a column from the Chicago Tribune commenting on the number of growing Confederates in Congress.[23] But her eyes kept returning to the W&A Train timetable: 8:42 AM arrival.

She glimpsed up over the top of the newspaper to watch a growing crowd, even in this bitter weather, forming to welcome the train. It had long become a ritual for the citizens to gather to see just who might disembark from each passenger train to visit their fair town. Today, the crowd was expected to be larger than usual, as word had leaked out about the arrival of Sheriff Otho Pierce from the town of Big Shanty, hauling his gypsy prisoner in tow.

Soon, Sheriff Goff and Clay came out of the jailhouse office and walked up to her.

"Look here, Clay," Goff said mockingly, "Deekie's not even frozen solid yet."

"Why don't ya' go inside, Deeks," her Virgil said, "git yerself warmed back up. Ya' been out here fer a spell."

"No, Virgil," she responded, "I think I'll come with ya' and the sheriff to welcome the train." She wanted to say how the sting of the December morning air was so much less biting than the full misery she felt she deserved, but preferred to not have her interior pain exposed outright. She would rather nurture it in her bosom, like some wayward wild creature, until it grew in rage and manifested itself explosively. That was so much more her style.

---

[23] All actual front page articles of the December 23, 1875 issue of "The Cartersville Express."

"Who's minding the gypsy woman," Deekie asked.

"We ain't but walkin' across the square to the depot, Deekie," Goff said, "but rest yer soul, Deputy Gilmore come in after ya' walked out into this cold."

"I reckon she'd be in better hands left alone than to have Howard watchin' over her," Deekie scoffed.

"Yer more than welcome to go inside and make sure my deputy tends to our prisoner's needs." Goff chided her.

"I done told ya'," Deekie replied, "I'm comin' with y'all." After her having said this, she walked right alongside them, and with Sheriff Goff leading the way, pressed through the collected crowd and up onto the platform.

Deekie stared down the tracks to the south. They seemed to twist away in a spiraling dance until small curls of a deep gray coal smoke could be made out in the distance. Soon, this visual was conjoined with the chug-chug-chug rhythm of the engine, pierced only periodically by the high-pitched screams of the whistle.

A total of six people disembarked, with two pairs of travelers preceding and following the sheriff of Big Shanty, Otho Pierce, and his prisoner. Deekie was surprised that the gypsy man was as old as he was, easily some two decades older than the woman in the jail cell. For some reason she was expecting a man more of the gypsy mother's same age, perhaps her very husband. Instead, the face of the man with Sheriff Pierce was gaunt with thin graying hair whose original color was betrayed by a thick black mustache.

"Good Morning, Otho," Sheriff Goff said, extending his hand. "Thank ya' fer coming up the road a spell to Cartersville."

"My pleasure, Alpheus," the Big Shanty Sheriff replied, "but I apologize for having to come over the Christmas holiday. I hate to be such a nuisance for ya' and Myrtle."

Deekie elbowed the ribs of her Virgil. They had greeted each other by their Christian names! Little did they know it would be the last time they did so in public

As they pressed through the crowd toward the jailhouse, it parted like the Red Sea. The fact that Sheriff Pierce had the gypsy fella handcuffed to himself gave the watchers a sense of danger. In reality, they were only employed to keep the gypsy man from slipping off to rejoin his caravan.

"Sheriff Goff," the Big Shanty Sheriff said, "How are ya' gonna know what this man tells ya' is actually what yer captive gypsy woman is sayin'? He could make up anything and we would never know fer sure if it were true."

"Day after Christmas, Sheriff Pierce," Goff replied, "I got two professors from Franklin College comin' in. One of them claims to be somewhat fluent in their language, at least enough to be able to confirm what yer prisoner tells us is told true. Now I figure we can use him to question the woman today, and tomorrow you, Myrtle and me will have a fine Christmas dinner at my house. On Sunday, we'll receive them two professors to confirm the statement she gave us through him (Goff pointed at the gypsy prisoner at that point) and Monday we can brief the judge. With a li'l luck by late Tuesday a after noon or so all parties can return to their homes to git ready for a festive New Years."

"And ya' don't think you'll need us to stay 'round fer yer court case?" Sheriff Pierce asked.

"No, Sheriff Pierce, that starts Tuesday, and so long as we have a witnessed, transcribed statement, Judge Ferris reckons that will suffice."

"Alrighty, then," Sheriff Pierce said, "let's git to it."

When the small entourage entered the jailhouse, Clay was surprised to see his brother there awaiting them all. Truitt explained that Judge Ferris had assigned him the duty to witness and record the translated testimony.

"I thought Judge Ferris was keepin' ya' at an arm's length from this case," Clay said.

"Funny to be hearin' ya' usin' that phrase, Clay" Truitt said. "Fact is with the holiday upon us there was no one else left to play this role. So here I am."

"Clay and Deekie," Sheriff Goff interrupted, "I am gonna have to respectfully ask ya' both to leave while we conduct this questionin'. And please take the li'l one with y'all. We got the business of the law to attend to."

So Clay and Deekie stepped outside with Li'l Miss Essie all bundled up tight, knowing that Truitt would later share what was revealed with them over dinner. He was not supposed to, but they always took a bit of entertainment at the table with his stories from the courthouse.

"Virgil," she said, "here is a dollar from my pay. Now go and get me a beautiful Christmas tree like all them fancy fine folks have in their homes. Drag it back to our spread. I'm goin' over to the general store and buy one of them stands fer it."

"C'mon now, Deeks," he argued, "we don't need no fancy tree. That dollar can be put to so much better use. Same with what you'll pay for that stand."

"Look here, Virgil," Deekie said, "This is likely the only time we'll have a Christmas with a little one and I am fixin' on doing it up right. Now do as I say."

"That chil' is too young to ever know the difference," Clay argued.

"We ain't doin' it fer her," Deekie said, "We're doing it fer me. Only time I'll ever have a baby in the house, I want it done up right. The memories of these next few days are gonna have to last me a lifetime. So please stop fussin' with me and jus' do as I say, Virgil."

Chapter Twenty-two

The Revelation

Deekie spent the rest of the day preparing for Christmas. She bought the stand for the tree and had enough left over to procure garland and thread to string popcorn. When her Virgil brought the tree up to the porch, she inspected it like the Mayor of Cartersville himself was coming to see it. Of course he wasn't, but nonetheless Deekie declared it to be a lovely tree and had her Virgil drag it inside.

They waited until Truitt came home to assist his brother in placing it in the stand. Having but the one arm, Clay told Deekie the damn contraption was "worse than settin' a fox trap." Soon enough with Truitt's help, the tree was freestanding in the open corner just past the fireplace.

Deekie had fried off some chicken for dinner along with greens, and after eating, as the three of them reposed at the table, she began to ask about the day's questioning.

"First off, Truitt," she said, "I am a might anxious to hear what that gypsy mama had to say fer herself. Did ya' git my two main questions answered?

"Come on, now, Deekie," he protested, "ya' know I am not supposed to be sharing this with y'all."

Truitt always began this way when they talked over the day's court cases at the table. She thought it made him feel important, so she would coax him to tell her just a little, and after getting started he would spew out everything. But today was too urgent on her mind to play along.

"Oh shush," she said to him. "You, me, Virgil and even Li'l Miss Essie know yer gonna spill yer guts. Now let's git on with it."

"Well, first off, her name ain't Miss Essie," Truitt said in pure retribution. "It's *Damara.* It means *'gentle little one.'* I think I have grown to like Li'l Miss Essie more, myself."

"Well, I'll be!" Deekie exclaimed. "I'll keep callin' her Li'l Miss Essie then, but Damara sounds ever so sweet. And what about her mama?"

"Her name is *'Vadoma.'* She said she was named after her father, *'Vadim.'* Oddly enough, both names mean 'to know.' Or at least that's what *Hanzi* says."

"And jus' who is Hanzi?" Clay asked.

"The only gypsy left, Clay," Truitt said, "the old translator Sheriff Pierce brought along. Vadoma knew him. They are both from the same tribe."

"So what exactly did this *Vadoma* know?" Deekie prodded.

"Well, it's a far sight different that what Herr Schilling claimed to have happened," Truitt said. "Vadoma said she and her child, Damara," Truit tilted his head toward the sleeping Miss Essie, "got separated from their group of gypsies in the woods as they were heading south. Oh, yeah, they call themselves *'Roma,'* not gypsies."

"So her *Roma* people jus' left 'em?" asked Deekie

"Vadoma said they likely didn't know she was missing right away. Sometimes she would travel with her *sisters* - other Roma women in their wagons. When she couldn't find her way back to the wagon train, she got worried and walked into town. She was on the street for two days, starvin', when she got the idea to steal the roses and sell them. It worked, but the next time she did so, Miss Margaret caught her outright, but when the old lady saw the baby, she took them both in. Vadoma was sure her husband would come back for her, but until then she was happy to stay with Miss Margaret a spell."

"So what 'zactly happened to Miss Margaret, according to her?" Clay asked.

"That's a bit of a long tale," Truitt began. "First off, Miss Margaret was always fighting with the Hun, as she called Schilling. Vadoma could not tell over what until one of Miss Margaret's stray dogs turned up dead. Then they really went at it. Also, some of her flowers were dying off, and that really sent the old woman off to argue with the Hun - again Vadoma's words."

"But this Vadoma didn't speak any English... How'd she know?" asked Deekie.

"She saw the dead dog and the wilted flowers and how mad Miss Margaret got," Truitt said. "I guess it don't take to needin' to speak a language when somebody gits that worked up over somethin'. But she said it seemed like these two had been fightin' with each other for a long time - she said long before she ever got there. So she sensed, anyway."

"What about the night Miss Margaret died?"

"Vadoma said Miss Margaret was always spyin' on that Hun. Every time he would go to work in his shed across the little creek, she would go out and try to see what he was doin' in there. On the night she died, she had walked right up and into his workshed and started screamin' at him. The German came out with a round ball of glass in his hand, with somethin' inside it. He waved it at her in an angry way. She watched this from a distance, but got scared so she went inside Miss Margaret's house and took Damara in her arms to the sofa. A few minutes later she heard a gut-wrenchin' scream, then all was quiet. After which, the German - the Hun, as she kept callin' him - the Hun came in the house and grabbed her. He took the baby from her and laid it in the basket on the sofa. Then he dragged Vadoma to the li'l creek where Miss Margaret laid still with blood pourin' outta her head. Vadoma said her face was covered in a clear liquid something like thick water. That was her description - thick water. She could not tell if Miss Margaret was dead or jus' layin' there hurt, but she was not movin'. Then the Hun picked up a rock and smeared it in the old woman's blood and placed it in her hand by force. When she dropped it right away, he took her arm and dragged her right into Miss Margaret's blood."

"How did she git away from him?" Clay asked.

"The Hun, as Vadoma called Schilling, stood her up and with the bloody rock still in her one arm, forced her to walk. That was when that second stray dog came by. Miss Margaret had been feedin' both animals. The first one died days earlier. This one come over and licked the clear thick water off Miss Margaret's face, tryin' to revive her like."

"So that's why Miss Margaret's face powder was all smeared so," observed Deekie.

"And why there jus' such little blood on her face," Clay added.

Truitt continued, "When Schilling went to kick it, the dog reared up, and bit him in the leg. That was when he let go of Vadoma and she ran. She feared if she ran back to get her baby, the Hun might hurt her Damara. So she ran away from Schilling, who chased her down on the Cassville Road. Soon afterward, the crowd started gatherin' and the one armed man, as she referred to Clay, showed up. She was scared for her life, until he fired the gun in the air and then the sheriff arrived. She went on to describe the rest of the night, but y'all were there for most of that."

"Truitt," Deekie said, "was she sore at me for taking' her baby?"

"Nope," he answered plainly. "She said ya' were the reason she was able to return to get her Damara. And she knew she couldn't keep her daughter in the jailhouse, so she was glad a kind soul like yourself had taken such good care of her. She said she blessed you."

"And here I thought she cursed me, all along," Deekie said in a relieved breath.

"Now the only question is how much of all that is true?" Clay said. "But that account answers a lot of questions."

"How so?" asked Truitt.

"Well," his brother offered, "that rock offered by Schilling was not likely what opened up that gash on Miss Margaret's head. But a piece of broken glass could. In fact, the undertaker took a piece of curved glass out from under her ripped open scalp. This gypsy woman…"

"Vadoma," Deekie corrected him.

"Okay, Vadoma," Clay conceded, "said Schilling waved around a piece of round glass. It fits that he may have used it to smash her head in. And the fact that the German Schilling dragged her from the front parlor explains the broad smeared trail comin' from the house that didn't go quite all the way up to Miss Margaret's body. Finally, jus' as Deekie said, this Vadoma saying that dog licked the face of Miss Margaret explains why her face powder was so smeared up. Deeks, 'member? That night ya' said it was like she had been takin' it off, but it wasn't her takin' it off, it was the dog's tongue doin' it."

"So ya' reckon Schilling killed her in a fit of rage and tried to make it look like Vadoma done it?" Truitt asked.

"That's the gist of it," Clay said.

"Could be a hard story for a jury to swaller," Truitt said. "What were they even fightin' over? Why would Schilling strike her with a ball of glass?"

"That don't matter much to Miss Margaret now, does it?" Deekie said.

"No, but sure as the day is long it will to a jury," countered Truitt. "Besides, who's gonna believe the word of a gypsy woman over that of a German businessman in town here?"

"I guess we're gonna find out next week," Clay said.

Chapter Twenty-three

Christmas Day

Clay and Deekie, and for that matter Truitt, were not the church-going types, but they certainly believed in the Good Book and its teachings. So on Christmas morning, they gathered by the hearth and sat in front of a roaring fire. Clay read out loud from Holy Scripture about the birth of Our Lord. Then, they settled down to a nice hearty breakfast, after which, when Li'l Miss Essie, or Damara, was awake, the three sang Christmas songs aloud.

The fire in the hearth warmed them all, protecting them from the freezing overnight conditions. Perhaps it was this toasty cabin warmth that fooled Deekie, for when she went outside to grab the metal pail for cleaning up the kitchen, she was shocked to see the water left in it overnight was frozen solid. A panic ran through her, as she had decided to leave Clay's gift out hidden in the roots of the tree so he would not find it. She feared the liquid in the snow globe also had frozen solid and that the glass might even had cracked ruining it forever. She ran from the porch down to the tree to clear away the pine straw that covered the recess in which she had hidden it.

As she pulled it from its berth, Deekie was ever so relieved to see it was in pristine condition. This was despite the glass being so cold she could hardly bear to hold it.

Why hadn't the water in it frozen? she wondered. In any case, she was very, very happy. She could not wait to present her gift to Clay. She shook the globe and a blizzard erupted, just as she had hoped. She couldn't wait to see his face the first time he made it snow.

Deekie ran as fast as she could back to the cabin - partially because of the excitement of her gift for her Virgil, but perhaps more truly driven by the bite of the cold December air. Before she entered, she hid the snow globe behind her back. Then she casually waltzed inside, laid the gift under the tree and draped a cleaning rag over top of it.

"Virgil, I have a li'l Christmas gift fer ya', my darlin'," she called out.

"And I fer ya' as well, Deeks," he whispered in her ear. She did not know he had snuck up behind her. When she turned around, she saw he held a black piece of velvet cloth in his hand.

Deekie took the gift from his hand and slowly but excitedly unfolded the cloth until she saw the most beautiful stone she had ever seen. It was green, a brilliant hue of that color, with a small hole drilled through its narrowest end. Through that orifice was a piece of fishing line. She could not believe how beautiful the stone was. It caught the flickering firelight and seemed to break it down it into all the colors of the rainbow. She was amazed that he had thought of it.

"I have a confession to make," he said. "I never used that trade dollar ya' gave me fer this here tree. I went out and cut this down from our woods. Instead, I used that dollar to buy this stone fer ya. Sorry I couldn't fix ya' up with a proper chain, but I will in time."

"Aw, Virgil," Deekie said, "that don't matter none. How did ya' think of gettin' me somethin' so beautiful?"

"From yer book," he said. "From that Hunchback book ya' been readin' to me here and there."

"Really? How so?"

"Well, the gypsy girl's name is Esmeralda," he said. "It was only a quick explanation, but ya' said that name means *'The Emerald.'* Now I can't afford no fancy emeralds, but I figured if I bought ya' a nice piece of green quartz, it might remind ya' of yer Esmeralda, and more importantly y'always will have it to make ya' think of yer Li'l Miss Essie. Again, I'm sorry it couldn't be real."

These were some of the most beautiful words he had ever spoken to her. Tears flooded her eyes.

"Funny thing is, in the book, Esmeralda's amulet - that's the fancy word fer it - it weren't real neither, just' a piece of green glass. This is the best gift a girl could ever be given," Deekie said, before correcting herself to add, "well, besides givin' her a daughter or son of our own."

"I pray to the Lord for you every night for that, Deeks."

"No," she said, "for us, Virgil."

"I'm gonna open up that hole and pass a strand of leather through it, to keep that fishing line from cuttin' into yer pretty li'l neck. Next time I got some extra coin, I'll buy ya' that proper silver plate necklace, I swear."

"It's so pretty I'd be happy if it had only pig guts to put round my neck. Now come over here close and see what I got ya'. I am anxious to see your reaction to it." She took Clay's arm in her left hand.

She picked up the gift, shrouded as it was, and held it out in the palm of her right hand. Clay took it and used his thumb to swipe back the dirty cloth laying over it. When he pulled it free, he looked at the hand-carved village scene within it.

"It's nice," he said, followed by, "but what is it?"

"Shake it up," Deekie said.

Clay did so and the snow took to its mystical flight. His face lit up in a way she had not seen for years.

"Will ya' look at that," he said. "Where did y'ever find such a thing?"

"They are brand new," she explained. "It's called a snow globe. I got it from Mr. John T. Owen down at Sayre's Drug Store."

She decided not to ruin the moment by explaining it was made by those highly possible murderous hands of Herr Heinrich Schilling. Or that she had been caught by him in recovering it from his workshed. Or that it had been Schilling who had ransacked their cabin looking for it. No, all that would have simply stoked a fire in her Virgil that she knew was better off left unkindled.

Chapter Twenty-four

Christmas Night

Her Virgil spent the rest of the Christmas day playing with the snow globe, which pleased Deekie to no end. He seemed to become more and more transfixed with it as the afternoon stretched toward dusk, staring with a penetrating gaze into the swirling, buoyant snowflakes. He would watch as they ever so lazily settled out, coating the hand-carved village scene enclosed in the glass dome in a layer of purity and serenity that seemed to have evaded his life to that point. It was only then that Clay became convinced this day was just that, pure and serene.

After dinner, Deekie began to pull on her jacket and to wrap Li'l Miss Essie in her warmest blankets.

"Where on earth are ya' goin'?" Clay called out.

"I reckon with it bein' Christmas night and all, that gypsy mother, Miss Vadoma, might like to see her little Damara. She must be awful lonely tonight."

"Jus' the opposite," Truitt called in from his room, its door being wide open to allow in the cabin's heat. "She has company in the other cell, remember the gypsy Hanzi is with her now. Although the sheriffs thought it best to move them so the center cell was open between them."

"Jus' give me a minute to get my woolen overcoat on," Clay said, "and I'll go wit' ya'."

"No, Virgil," Deekie ignored her man, "yer better off stayin' here, we'll be fine. In fact, I did remember Hanzi, the gypsy interpreter was with her. This will give me the chance for the first time to have a conversation with Vadoma. I'd rather ya' not be listenin' to what I have to say to her. And we're likely to be there fer a good spell."

"Still, I can't have ya' walkin' the streets alone," Clay said.

"Virgil! It's Christmas night, who would dare bother us? Especially here in our peaceful town of Cartersville?"

"Ya' reckon that might have been one of Miss Margaret's last thoughts?" Clay responded.

"We will be fine," she demanded, "I love ya' Virgil, but if ya' come along you'll have ruined my best Christmas Day ever."

"How ya' fixin' to get in?" Clay asked.

"I done took care of that," Deekie answered. "Sheriff Goff gave me an office key should I want to visit over this weekend. I guess the man has a heart after all. But he wouldn't trust me with a key to her cell, so I guess we'll be talkin' and visitin' through the jail bars."

And with that, she began to leave the cabin, baby in arm, but having opened the door, she closed it as if another thought was rattling around within her.

"Virgil, can I ask a great favor of ya'?" Her voice was soft and caring, as if seeking to have her need satisfied.

"Sure, Deeks, anything…"

"Can I take that snow globe I gave ya' with me? It might be something nice for both them gypsies in that jailhouse to see, ya' know, to brighten their Christmas night."

"I don't see why not," he said, "if I keep lookin' on it much longer I jus' might end up inside that little wooden village. Somethin' 'bout it seems to draw me in, but I can't put a finger on it. Here take it. Can ya' carry all this?"

"Don't worry on that," she answered, "it fits right in my coat pocket. Nice and snug. I'll take good care of it."

He handed the Christmas gift to her, and she showed him how nicely it fit in her coat pocket, having no way to pop out less someone kicked her from behind and below, and that surely wouldn't be happening.

After she left with the child, Clay was left with a thought that so completely blanketed his mind it might as well been a fresh coating of snow settling out on that globe's alpine village. How he had wished his Maw was there to enjoy the simplicity of Deekie's gift. So he pulled on his woolen coat, and walked out to her grave to spend a few minutes with her while Deekie was gone. Deekie always accused her Virgil of still pining for his Maw. Since she had treated his Deekie so nastily while alive, it often led to the start of quarreling between them, despite the fact his Maw had been gone four several years by then.

Given that, the sting of the frigid night air seemed strangely appropriate. Clay held his hat in hand, as he bowed his head over his Maw's marker. He liked coming here because he would think on all that the poor woman had been through during her years, which somehow most often helped him to clear his own thoughts. Yet this night, his mind was still a tangle of thickets. Despite the solitude, it failed to unwind. His mind just would not clear.

Something nipped at his mind's peace like a wild animal, but he could not put his finger exactly on what it was. He could not make it out, as if it were hidden in the darkness waiting to strike. Yet still, Clay sensed a threat out there, stalking them all - himself, Truitt and Deekie.

Clay hung his head over his Maw's grave. It felt like that first night of December when he bowed his head over Colonel Tumlin's crypt. He felt fresh his concern for the coyotes along the creek that sent him walking the long way round down along the Cassville Road. He thought on being drawn to that raucous crowd as it formed around Schilling and the gypsy gal. He recalled as the sun came up seeing in its soft diffused light the dead body of old Miss Margaret, and the harsh savagery done to her head. Then he thought of that dead dog laying atop her cold body, as if trying to warm her back to life. Looking down at his Maw's grave, he prayed she could not feel the eternal cold.

Clay remembered his Maw, and the many hours she'd spend with her sewing basket warming herself by the fire. Her sewing basket - that was it! Clay blessed himself and raced into the house. Without so much as taking off his coat, he rifled through his Maw's sewing basket until he found the rolled-up piece of black felt. He took it to the table and carefully unfurled it. He gazed upon those white specks dotted across its darkness. He realized this was the answer. These were the flakes of snow in his Deekie's gift - the snow in her globe. He recalled Sheriff Goff saying how Schilling was a glassblower. Clay was sure then that the gypsy Vadoma's version of that night must be true. Herr Schilling had smashed in Miss Margaret's head with a snow globe. He knew in his bones that Schilling was the threat nipping at his mind's ease. He cursed himself for letting Deekie take Li'l Essie to the town square all alone.

Deekie crested the hill and found herself between the Gilreath Cottage and the Cartersville Baptist Church just across the street. It was unusually quiet, with all the Christmas services by then long over.

The cold was stinging more than she could bear, so Deekie, with more concern for the child than herself, decided to try the church door. She did so and found it unlocked, as she suspected it might be. She walked in to warm herself and the infant. In the shadow of the cross above, she coddled Li'l Miss Essie one last time, knowing it might be one of their last few moments alone together.

After those few warming minutes, they pressed on over the hill and down onto the town square. She thought on Sheriff Goff and Sheriff Pierce as she unlocked the door to the jailhouse. She wondered if they enjoyed their Christmas meal together, while the two gypsies remained locked up together, away from their families, their people, and their way of life.

The office was warm and on the sheriff's desk sat the plates, cutlery and remains of the food someone had served them for Christmas dinner. So, as she hoped, they had not been entirely forgotten after all.

Vadoma leapt from the cot and rushed to the bars of her cell as soon as she heard the key engage the lock of the office door. She cried out the name Damara over and over again, as she had each time that Deekie brought the young girl back to her. However, Deekie previously had heard only gibberish, but this time she recognized the plaintiff cry of a mother desperate only to hold her child once more.

Deekie brought the infant over to the cells. As Truitt had mentioned, Vadoma, who had been previously in the center cell, was moved to the corner on Deekie's left. The old man, Hanzi, was in the far right cell. The center was left empty, as a sort of buffer between the two, as if somehow that might keep them from conspiring. But conspiracies are crafted from thoughts and words, and the empty space could not preclude the transfer of either.

Deekie realized that she had calculated correctly in one regard. Without anyone present, there was no way to unlock the cell door. So she awkwardly stood a few feet away from the bars, through which the mother's arms penetrated in a pleading sway. Then more guttural words tripped from the woman's tongue, and Deekie was once again left understanding none of it.

"She says *'come closer, I need my daughter'*," Hanzi explained. It was the first time Deekie had heard him speak. His English was thickly layered with an accent she had never heard before. It took Deekie a few seconds to rip away those ragged edges so that she could understand the meaning of his words.

"Yes, of course," she responded, and stepped as close to the bars as she could without crushing the child. Li'l Miss Essie became Damara as soon as she was laid in her mother's outstretched palms, a transformation that Deekie had always seen. She knew that she herself could never love the child as fully as its mother did. This was obvious in the grinning face and warm reaction of the babe.

"So why don't she speak English like ya' do?'" Deekie asked.

"She only came to us recently from Spain," he said.

"Then why come here," she asked. "Why not stay with her people there."

"Because her husband was wanted there for murder," Hanzi said. "But he did not do it, so they came to join us here in America. Now, all this happens here!"

Vadoma said something in their tongue.

"She says you are such a wonderful woman for bringing Damara to her on Christmas night," Hanzi explained. "And she thanks you for caring for her child when she herself could not."

"Well, it was all I could do," Deekie explained as Hanzi translated her words. "'Specially after all that she's been through, held wrongly fer murder like her husband."

"I did not kill that woman," Vadoma said through Hanzi, "and yet they treat me like a dog. I could never hurt that woman who herself fed us and sheltered my child."

Deekie felt a bout of extreme guilt pulse through her. She wondered if Vadoma knew how selfishly she had hoped to keep her daughter, even secretly convicting the gypsy woman in her mind early on to make it possible.

Vadoma held the child as close as she could with the harsh reality of the iron bars between them. The caress was so loving despite the hardened steel rods that Deekie knew she must somehow make the child's visit easier.

"Tell her to hold her on her own for a minute," Deekie told Hanzi, who then sprayed a tangle of gypsy words to Vadoma. Deekie went back to the sheriff's desk and pulled his chair up to the cell. She then could sit opposite the child's mother, who had dropped to her knees to play through its bars with her daughter atop Deekie's lap.

"She says again you are wonderful," Hanzi relayed. Like a magician he conjured the English from the stream of babbles coming from Vadoma's lips. "She says you have taken such good care of her Damara. You will make a fine mother one day."

Deekie's head dropped upon hearing this. Despite trying over and over and over again, she had come to the conclusion that for whatever reason, she and Virgil would never have a li'l one.

Deekie wanted the gypsy mother's words to be true so badly that her heart ached. Vadoma's simplest touch had cut through her every emotion well before Hanzi had ever been there. There was in that first kiss by Vadoma on her forehead all the thanks that she would ever need.

The gypsy woman held her daughter with a single hand while she pushed her other arm through the bars to grasp Deekie's face. At the moment that her palm cupped her cheek, a flash sparked wildly again within Deekie. She once more saw the image of herself nursing a child, her own child. A wave of indescribably delicate pleasure overcame her. She felt satisfaction, total satisfaction.

After a bit, Deekie collected herself. She remembered Clay's Christmas gift that she brought to amuse these gypsies.

"I have something to show ya' that I think ya' will enjoy," she told Hanzi. Then she reached in her pocket and produced the snow globe, shaking it wildly as she did so.

Vadoma pulled back into the cell, shrieking, leaving her daughter in Deekie's lap. She fell back on her arms, her legs still tucked under her. Fear painted her face. From her lips came forth a stream of rushed, excited gibberish.

"No, no. It's okay," Deekie pleaded for Hanzi to translate. "It's jus' a toy."

"She says it is what the Hun used to kill the old woman," Hanzi replied. "She begs you to put it away. It is evil, like the Hun himself. Put it away."

"Pliss, Pliss," Vadoma pleaded in English.

Deekie returned the globe to the pocket of her coat. She was amazed at how forcibly the woman had reacted.

"She says to get rid of it," Hanzi warned. "Do not play with trinkets that have been cursed in the shadow of death. Rid yourself of this *thing.*"

"I'm sorry," Deekie muttered. "I only meant to please ya' both. I thought it might make ya' happy." She slipped the bauble back into her pocket.

"What will make me happy is to leave this cell, this town, so I can rejoin my people," Hanzi translated for her.

A heavy silence befell the office. It was painful for Deekie, who felt embarrassed. She had ruined a beautiful moment of Christmas reunion between a mother and her daughter. So she sat there awkward as a scolded child as she continued to let Vadoma to care for her child through the bars. This went on for another half hour, before Deekie could bear no more and declared, "It's about time fer us to git goin' on our way."

The mother stood after hearing the translation of her visitor's words. Deekie then stood herself up to hand the infant back to her mother's arms extended through the bars of the cell. After returning the chair to the sheriff's desk, Deekie took the child from Vadoma's arms. Hanzi translated the gypsy mother's final words.

"Vadoma says you are a good woman. You care not only for her Damara, but for herself as well. God will bless you for this. But she warns do not take joy in the trinkets of death. They are often disguised by the devil to appeal to the unsuspecting. Rid yourself of them."

Deekie thought the woman to have been crazed by witnessing Miss Margaret's corpse. It was understandable, but how could keeping a simple snow globe bring Deekie harm? She would return it to Virgil despite it having been made by the blood-stained hands of Heinrich Schilling.

Chapter Twenty-five

Sanctuary

The night's visit had been marred by the gypsy woman Vadoma's reaction to the snow globe. Instead of being pleased with the novelty of it, she was revolted by its presence. Deekie left the sheriff's office and jailhouse hurriedly, but made sure to lock the door on her way out. As soon as she did the night's chill clawed at her back. Soon the clack of her footsteps resounded throughout the empty square.

Deekie climbed the hill as Market Street rose just beyond the train depot, but had a most unsettled feeling as she did so. She looked around several times, sensing but never spotting what she felt to be a figure lurking behind her. She was sure something or someone was there, and at this point wished terribly that Sheriff Goff had never taken her Colt Navy Six from her. She felt exposed, vulnerable. Most of all, a building panic raced in her heart, against which she carried the gypsy's child, Damara, who she knew she had no real means of protecting.

Deekie scuttled along the dark empty street, as everyone remained inside enjoying their Christmas revelries. She was now certain someone was following her. The wait to be suddenly overtaken physically was rattling her nerves. Despite being in the open, she felt trapped. She became desperate for an escape from her situation.

Deekie came to the Cartersville Baptist Church, just opposite the Gilreath Cottage. Recalling the church having been open earlier, Deekie climbed its steps with the infant and pushed the door open to take shelter within. She thought to herself, *I'll remain here until the threat passes, certainly we'll be safe here.*

Upon entering, she looked for a lock to throw, but was terrified to find it could only be locked with a key. She clutched at the child protectively, and scanned the vestibule to see if there was anything she could push up against the door to barricade herself and the child in. See saw a large free-standing cabinet that might provide enough resistance. Deekie found a bench in the church and was preparing to lay down the child so she could use both hands to move the cabinet. Yet, as she did, the door to the church was pushed open from outside.

Deekie stopped herself in the middle of laying down the child, clutched the infant to her chest and walked slowly backward toward the front of the church. Her nerves jumped within in her as a massive, bearded figure emerged into the shadowy vestibule. There was no mistaking the threatening likeness of Heinrich Schilling as he came in from the cold.

"Miss Deekie," he called to her, "do not be afraid. I merely want you to give me the *Schneekugel* you took from my workshed. The snow globe, that is."

"I don't have it," she screamed at him, "now leave me alone."

"Ahh, but you do have it," he said. "I *vatched* you in the sheriff's office as you showed it to that gypsy *Hexe*. I *vatched* from *der vindow* outside on the square."

"I said leave me alone," Deekie screamed, causing the child to abruptly begin to cry. "It's mine. I paid fer it. Yer'll never get it back."

The German walked slowly forward toward her. His right arm was held slightly behind his back. She worried what he hid from her there.

"*Ya*, I *vill* take it," he said, bringing his arm forward and revealing the same iron rod he had threatened her with in the workshed. "Do you know in German *ve* have the saying, *'Aus Schaden wird man klug.'* It means, *from failure a man can be made smart.* That *Schneekugel* you have *vas* one of the first I made, in the fact the very last one of the first batch I ever made. It needs to be fixed. Had you left it *vith* me, I *vould* have fixed it and returned it to you by now. Instead, you threatened me with your gun."

"And I got it with me, Herr Schillin'," she lied as she reached inside her coat. "Come another step toward us and I'll give ya' another look of it."

The baby wailed, its cries cut through the peace of the empty church like a siren of impending doom.

"*Nein,* you do not," the German said. "I complained to *da* judge and *da* sheriff took the *veapon* from you. I know this. Now, Miss Deekie, you *vill* give me that bit of my glass *vork* from out of your pocket, please."

Deekie did not know what to say. She backed away from him until she stood under the plain wooden cross suspended over the front altar of the house of worship. Then, almost as an afterthought, she muttered out on a half breath the single, solitary word,

"Sanctuary."

The German stopped in his tracks. *"Vhat* do you mean by saying *dis vord, 'Sanctuary'?"*

"This is a house of God," Deekie declared boldly. "It's a sanctuary from all evil."

Schilling took another step forward, still patting the iron rod harshly against his palm. "So, you think me *teuflisch, eh*? Evil, as you *vould* say?"

"Don't ya' come any closer," she said, pointing the hand hidden in her pocket at him. "I have my Virgil's gun, and I'll use it. I know ya' killed Miss Margaret. I'm still not right sure why, but I know ya' did. And I know why ya' want it so bad, because it's somehow linked to Miss Margaret's death. Well, yer not gettin' it. Not lessen yer ready to kill fer it. Here in the sanctuary of God's house."

He walked very slowly toward her and the crying child. "Miss Deekie," he said, "I have never killed anyone..."

She screamed at him, "Liar!"

"... that did not deserve it. In my country we have another saying, *'Krummes Holz gibt auch gerades Feuer.'* It means even crooked logs make straight fire. Thus, you remain a crooked log, forcing me to do what I must do to make a straight fire. I am sorry."

Then he moved toward her with an offensive lurch of energy, and Deekie screamed as she backed away. "No!"

As Schilling raised the iron bar overhead to strike at her with his right hand, he grasped the high back of the front row of wooden benches with his left hand to steady himself. She saw this and again screamed out with every bit of energy she could muster, "NO!!!"

Deekie reactively dropped her butt to the floor, and crouched forward to protect the wailing infant from the expected blow.

That blow never fell. Schilling spared the rod, and as he did so, reached down toward the child. Deekie screamed once more, clutching Damara as tightly as she could to her bosom, to protect the child from the hands of the Hun. Instead, those hands reached into the pocket of Deekie's coat and extracted the snow globe. He stood smiling victorious over her, and let out a sinister snicker.

"Dis is all you *hadt* to do, Miss Deekie, to give me *vhat* I *vanted,"* he mused as she lay with the crying infant at his feet. "Now, *vhat shouldt* I do *vith* the both of you?"

That was when his question was answered with nothing more than a single metallic click, as simple as the chirp of a single cricket.

"I think ya' done enough already, Herr Schilling," Clay called out moments later from the back of the church. Behind him the door from the street remained only partially closed, betraying his recent and rapid entry.

"Thank God yer here, Virgil," Deekie screamed out from lying on her back at the feet of the German.

"Best to thank the Lord he gave ya' such a loud mouth," Clay answered. "I had jus' walked past on my way to Sheriff Goff's office when I heard yer scream."

Schilling, still holding the snow globe, slowly turned to face Clay. As he did, he saw the Navy Six in Clay's only hand pointed at him, it's hammer drawn back, which he knew from his Prussian military training meant he was only a twitch away from being shot.

"How dare you point your *veapon* at me," he exclaimed. "Judge Ferris *vill* have many questions for you and *der* sheriff…*vhy* did he not take both your pistols?"

"I think the only question to be answered," Clay said, "is why yer wantin' that damn snow globe back so badly. What is it about that trinket that would make yer risk threatening my woman and that innocent child so. Now git away from them both."

Schilling followed his order and moved away from Deekie and the still wailing infant. However, as he did so he tried to hide the fact that he had drawn back the iron rod in order to strike at and break the glass of the snow globe.

A loud explosion rang out from the back of the sanctuary. The wood of the bench back closest to the German splintered into the air with explosive force. The echo of the gunshot resonated through the empty space, but was quickly replaced by the sulfurous smell of gunpowder. The surprise of the firing froze Schilling in his tracks.

"I ain't afraid to use this gun," Clay warned from the back of the church. "Now, Herr Schilling, I have killed many a man in my life, but I have never done so in any house of God before. I would like to be able to continue to say that in the future and fer it to be told true. So jus' go ahead and drop that rod ya' got there. Nice and slow like."

Schilling did lower his arm and released the iron rod, which fell to the floor with a solid thud of defeat.

"You do not *understandt*, Mr. Clay. I never had any intention to strike at your *voman* or the child. *I yust vanted* to frighten them, *yust* so I could collect my *Schneekugel*. It is not made right. It needs to be *revorked.* My hands made it, so it is rightfully mine to do *vith* as I please."

"Nope, Heinrich, as of today, that snow globe is mine," Clay said as he walked up the main aisle toward the German, "I think I'll give that toy to Sheriff Goff. Like I said, he'll be best to decide jus' why yer' wantin' it back so bad that ya' would attack a defenseless woman and child inside an empty church on Christmas night."

Clay called out to Deekie, who by then had stood upright with the child. "Deeks, can ya' take that snow globe from him? With me holdin' this Colt Navy, I am jus' a bit short-handed here."

Deekie walked up next to the German. She knew not to stand in the line of sight between him and her Virgil. She stood beside the Hun. She was nonetheless still careful that he might lash out at her or the child. Yet she knew if he did, her Virgil would strike him down in an instant, before any harm could befall either of them. She reached her hand out beside Schilling for him to place the snow globe in it.

Schilling did as her motion requested, but he had one last bit of trickery up his sleeve. He intentionally dropped the item onto the edge of her upturned hand instead of into its open palm. The glass globe rolled off and fell to the floor. Deekie, caught off guard by the German's move, reacted in two ways. First she had tried to grasp it but knew she could not. Instinctively, she kicked out her leg, and instead of the glass crashing hard onto the wooden floor of the church, it first struck the softly worn and tattered leather of Deekie's boot. The result was the globe bounced off and rolled a bit before it's base prevented it from traveling much further, but it remained intact.

Herr Heinrich muttered what Clay took to be a curse word in German under his breath. He seemed to resign himself now to his utter defeat.

"Go ahead and fetch it, Deeks. I got him covered."

Deekie walked a wide path around Schilling and retrieved the rattled but otherwise undisturbed globe. She raised it to watch a flurry of white flakes swirl in commotion over the village inside.

"It looks to be in one piece," she called out to Clay.

Just then the Reverend of the church appeared inside the door in the vestibule. He scanned the inside of his domain intently. "What on earth is going on in here? Was that a gunshot I heard inside this church?"

"Sorry 'bout that, Pastor," Clay said still brandishing the Colt Navy Six, "but can ya' have someone go and roust up Sheriff Goff fer me? We have a little situation to deal with here."

"What in the name of Judas happened to that benchback?" the Reverend asked agitatedly, pointing to the splintered remains of the front row seat.

Clay responded with a wry grin, "Jus' a little of what ya' might call divine intervention. Jus' 'nuff so to keep sacred yer Sanctuary!"

Chapter Twenty-six

Saint Stephen's Day

That Christmas evening, Clay detained Herr Heinrich Schilling until Sheriff Goff came from his home to take the German into custody. Goff was accompanied by his holiday guest, Sheriff Otho Pierce from the town of Big Shanty. Schilling's iron rod was retrieved from the church and preserved as evidence. He was otherwise found to be unarmed.

"Tomorrow, I will have separate accommodations for the German," Goff said to Sheriff Pierce, "but would it offend ya' if I were to place yer gypsy man in the center cell to keep Schilling away from that gypsy gal overnight. Otherwise she's likely to become hysterical, findin' herself within his reach, even though I intend to gag and cuff him until I move him to the courthouse holding cell at dawn."

"That's finer than a frog's hair to me," Sheriff Pierce said. "What are ya' gonna hold him for?"

"Fer about a few days, I reckon," Goff responded, "at least until Judge Ferris figures out if he still wants to go forward with this gypsy gal's trial. We got that couple of professors comin' in on the train tomorrow from Franklin College to help us get all this business sorted out. Maybe ya' and yer prisoner can return home on the Tuesday train."

"Naw, I meant what ya' gonna charge him with?" Sheriff Pierce clarified.

"Well, I'm thinkin' fer sheer stupidity fer starters," Goff said. "I mean who is thick enough to threaten a woman with an iron rod, holdin' a baby in a church on Christmas night? Then, maybe, I'll tack on reckless abandon, disturbin' the peace, and threatenin' civil battery."

"All based only on the testimony of the other two?" Pierce then added, "I mean the woman and the one-armed fella."

"They have names, Sheriff Pierce," Goff said, "Deekie and Clay. Their word's good 'nuff for me to hold Schilling. Who knows, if them two college professors are half as good as been said, maybe he's got a murder charge forthcomin' too."

"I thought ya' was jus' bringin' in the one of them, that highbrow for his language skills," said Sheriff Pierce.

"I was," Goff said, "but when I caught wind of the German cookin' up them chemicals in his workshed, I telegrammed Dr. Stevens to see if he could bring along an associate who might know somethin' 'bout chemistry. So, that's why that second professor is comin' to our li'l town."

"What made ya' do that?" Pierce asked. "I thought ya' said there was no still or anything there when ya' went into Schilling's shed."

Goff gave his visitor a glance that spoke volumes, one that was immediately recognized and understood by his fellow lawman.

"Nope. Weren't none," agreed Sheriff Goff. "But that hole in the wall kept botherin' at me."

"I see," said Pierce. "Left yer stomach feelin' a little uneasy, did it?"

"Sure did," admitted Goff. "It looked to be fer some kind of drain line. I thought he might be moonshinin' or brewing somethin' unlawful in there. When I went by later and that pipe was stickin' out, jus' as Deekie said durin' her visit, then I knew he was doin' somethin' he didn't want me knowin' bout. I thought on the dead woman, Miss Margaret, and how she complained one of her stray pups was found dead, and of her Christmas Roses dyin' off. I thought there might be a connection. Only thing was when I went through her hot house, all the roses seemed to be doin' jus' fine, not a one of them was wilted. But now, Clay says that the white flecks he scraped off the tongue of that second dead dog, the one from the murder scene, matched up with the flakes of snow globe. Well, it's all startin' to make sense. That dog licked the face of the dead woman. Somethin' the German was cookin' up in there for them snow globes was poisonin' them dogs. And he must have known it, 'nuff to collect up all them globes he sold and rework 'em. Empty 'em out and refill them back up. All 'cept for the one Deekie bought and took back from him."

The next day the two sheriffs waited on the arrival of the afternoon passenger train at the depot. Amongst others disembarking from it were two finely dressed gentlemen; one wore a dark gray silk suit and top hat, the other wore a less elegant outfit of brown trousers and a coarsely woven tweed jacket. The man in the suit was fully, but neatly, bearded and the jacketed one bore a tidy goatee.

"Those two Jim Dandies figure fer sure to be our college professors," Sheriff Goff said. "Ain't never before seen two men more out of their element than these two fellas here in town. I reckon the one wearin' the stove pipe on his head is our doctor of tongues, the other tweedy one likely to be the chemist." Both lawmen walked up to the two visitors and introduced themselves.

"We are most pleasantly appreciative to make your fine acquaintance, gentlemen," said the head under the top hat. "I am Dr. Robin Stevens, professor of languages. It is my great honor to present to you my colleague, Dr. Laurent Lavoisier, a direct descendant of the famous French chemist, Antoine Lavoisier."

"So it's Robin and Laura?" asked the befuddled Sheriff Otho Pierce, who secretly thought both to be women's names.

"Actually, it's not Laura, but Laurent," Dr. Stevens corrected the sheriff, once more not pronouncing the "t" in the French manner. "It's the Parisian variant of Lawrence. But, gentlemen, let's keep this professional, so feel free to address us as Doctor Stevens and Doctor Lavoisier."

"Well, Dr. Stevens," Goff said, a little put off by the direction given as to how to address the pair, "feel free to call me Sheriff Goff and this here's Sheriff Pierce from the town of Big Shanty, who himself is a direct descendant of the former President Franklin Pierce."

As soon as the lie left Goff's lips, Otho Pierce felt his fellow lawman's elbow gentle rattle his ribs, as if to say *that will teach them.* The group of four then braved the bitter cold and crossed the square over to Goff's office and jailhouse, which was on the corner adjacent to the courthouse.

Once inside they could talk freely, as Heinrich Schilling had earlier in the day been relocated to a holding cell in the courthouse.

"It should be quite easy for me to validate this woman's statement given that you have brought along this Romani interpreter," Dr. Stevens said to Sheriff Pierce.

"He ain't no Romanian, jus' a gypsy," Sheriff Pierce said, "no more than he ain't no interpreter either. He jus' tells us in English what she's sayin'."

The linguist gave the man a condescending look. "Not Romanian, *Romani.* It is the correct term for your term, *gypsy.* That term incorrectly assumed these wandering souls had come from Egypt, when in actuality they originated in the Indo-Persian subcontinent."

"That part about bein' from Egypt is exactly what Miss Deekie had read in that book," Sheriff Goff said.

"What book might that be?" Dr. Stevens asked.

"The Hunchback of Notre Dame," Goff answered.

"Ah, *Notre Dame de Paris* by Victor Hugo," Dr. Lavoisier corrected the sheriff's pronunciation. He rolled the "r" in Notre, and melded the *"dame"* into *"dom."* He breathed in slowly, as if attesting to some great interior knowledge. "Notre Dame de Paris! That is the title given by Hugo to his masterpiece. Only in America would such prominence be given to that grotesque equal of the gargoyles, the bell ringer Quasimodo, but the real protagonist of that novel is the Gothic Cathedral itself. Yes, that text is full of Romani characters, it is true."

Sheriff Alpheus T. Goff did not take kindly to being corrected in his own office by that French-loving chemist.

"That all may be true," Goff said, "but I seen that book and the title clearly says, *'The Hunchback of Notre Dame.'* And he calls these people *gypsies,* not *Romani,* clear throughout. The book was only writ a little over forty years ago. Anyway, I suggest we get down to business for a few hours, then we can check y'all into the Park Hotel."

For the next two hours, Dr. Stevens read over the transcript that Truitt had taken down from the questioning of the gypsy woman. He intermittently would ask questions directly of her in her native tongue. Occasionally the professor would stumble on a word or phrase and the gypsy elder, Hanzi, in the next cell would assist and clarify. Even given this, Doctor Stevens was ready after their time together to proclaim that the interpretation given by the man accurately reflected the gypsy woman's testimony.

While this was going on, Sheriff Goff answered questions that Dr. Lavoisier had regarding the snow globe. It had been taken by Goff the night before as evidence. While it had been intentionally dropped by the German Schilling, undoubtedly with the intention to crack its glass globe and spill out the solution inside, it remained virtually intact. The only evidence of mishandling was a slight leakage of fluid where the globe adjoined the base.

The professor of chemistry sat in the sheriff's chair and continually played with the globe, kicking up a swirling snowstorm within it. When he was told of the German's strong armed tactics to get hold of it, and then to try and break it open as if to drain out the fluid, the professor seemed extremely intrigued. As he handled the globe, the chemist would swipe the tip of his pinky finger over the small leakage around its base and very tentatively touch it to the tip of his tongue.

"So, Dr. Lavoisier," Goff asked after an extended period, "does any of this make any sense to you?"

"Perhaps," he mused, still watching a swirling storm inside of the glass globe slowly, indeed too sluggishly, settle out onto the village. "Just perhaps I understand what may be going on here."

"Would ya' like to explain it to me?"

"If I can," answered the chemist.

"Why would ya' not be able to?" Goff asked.

"Because you do not understand the science, but I will try."

"Well thank ya'. Yer words will git my full, if somewhat uneducated attention," Goff chided his guest.

"Sheriff Goff," Lavoisier said, "do you imbibe of alcohol? Whiskey or beer?"

"Of course," he quickly answered. "Don't know a lawman who don't. Both and often. Be lyin' if I said any different."

"Well, an alcohol, any alcohol, is simply a chemical compound with a single hydroxy group on it. An -OH sticking off the end of a chain of carbon atoms. Now, I assume you have heard of glycerin."

"Sure, I've heard of it. Not too sure what it is used fer." Goff gave the chemist a wanting look.

"It has been used in watercolor paints, ever since 1832 when William Winsor and Henry Newton - both men were chemists *and* painters - discovered its artistic properties. Here, taste the tiny amount of fluid I have on the tip of my small finger."

The professor held out his dabbed pinky finger but the sheriff drew back from it.

"Go ahead, taste it, in this small amount it is safe enough." Doctor Lavoisier stretched forward his hand.

The sheriff leaned forward and stuck out his tongue, and the professor quickly dotted his fingertip onto the exposed feature.

"Hmmmpff," Sheriff Goff said, "very sweet. Terribly sweet, in fact."

Then Dr. Lavoisier offered the same to Sheriff Pierce, only to be rejected. "I'll take Sheriff Goff's word on the taste of it."

"Suit yourself," the professor said. Then, turning back to Sheriff Goff he said, "Glycerin is sometimes called a triple alcohol. Every molecule has three of those -OH hydroxy groups, whereas alcohol only has one. The reason it is called glycerin is because of that very sweet taste. Comes from the ancient Greek word *'glukus'* which translates to sweet. Like water, it is a clear, odorless liquid, but much more viscous, that is thicker, than water would be. Could be what the German is filling these globes with. Notice how long it takes for the snow to settle out."

"Too long," Goff said, "I noticed that. Cuz of the liquid's thickness, right? Is it poisonous?"

"Not glycerin," Lavoisier said, but then laid out the rest of his supposition, "but there is a newer class of compounds that are considered to be double alcohols. Like glycerin they are sweet, and because of this are named *glycols*. They are also very clear, and very odorless, and keep water from freezing."

"Makes sense because Deekie's globe was hid outside over several nights and never froze up," Goff said.

"However, they are extremely toxic," the chemist added "Not only to humans, but especially to small animals like dogs. I think there is a possibility, just a theory mind you, that this German was making these glycols in his workshed. Some got washed out the drain and could have poisoned the first stray dog, bringing that Miss Margaret woman to extreme fury. If, as you think the German got into an argument with her and ended up striking her with the globe, the glycol would have covered her face. Perhaps she died of glycol poisoning. Most surely the second dog did, when it licked the sweet fluid from her face."

Then his colleague, Dr. Stevens yelled in from back near the cell, "And this woman testified that the dead woman's face was covered in what she called, for lack of a better term, *'thick water.'* That supports your theory."

"After the German had stoked up the crowd which you saved the gypsy woman from," Dr. Lavoisier said, "he knew he had to cover his tracks. That would explain why Schilling was so eager to get his hands on that last snow globe. He likely refilled the others with the non-toxic glycerin after draining out the poisonous glycol. That only left the snow globe Deekie had bought as containing the toxic fluid. It was the one last damning bit of evidence he must have direly wanted to destroy."

"Wait a minute," Sheriff Goff said, "how would this German know about all this chemistry and such?"

"Didn't you say he was a glassblower by trade?"

"Yup," Goff said, "what of it?"

"In Europe," the professor said, "the production of chemical glassware is very lucrative. All the rich aristocrats love to dabble in chemistry, and will pay dearly for custom made glass products. Your German likely knows a lot more chemistry than just this if he had been selling his custom made glasswares over there for very long. Funny thing is, these glycols were discovered in the Alsace region between Germany and France, so it is very likely that he might have known of them."

"Why would he not have just used the other stuff - the glycerine?" Sheriff Goff asked.

"Because the use of it in those artistic paints has driven the price way up," Professor Lavoisier said. "I presume Schilling likely makes the glycols on the cheap, but just wasn't aware of how poisonous those compounds truly are. Especially in concentrated form."

"Okay," Goff said. "How do we go ahead and test yer assumption?"

"Are there any assayers about?" Lavoisier asked.

"In Stegall's Station, that's a mining town, south of here," Goff said, "jus' a short piece down the road."

"Then they will have what it takes to test my theory," he said. "I will jus' need this," he held out Deekie's snow globe, "and one of the reworked globes. We can do it in an afternoon."

"First, I gotta run all this by Judge Ferris," Goff held out two arms. "In the meanwhile, I'll have my deputy go out and get his hands on one of them re-worked globes. If yer right, this young lady might, jus' might, have a much brighter future in front of her."

Chapter Twenty-seven

All was set. Judge Ferris was briefed on the arrest of Heinrich Schilling and agreed to delay the start of the gypsy's trial until the results of the testing of the snow globes was conducted. An assayer's office in Stegall's Station had been found that could test the fluids under the direction of Professor Lavoisier. There were any number of reworked globes to test, but only one of the original globes remained - Deekie's gift to her Virgil.

"They need yer say-so to test it," Clay informed her.

"I know, but I bought that snow globe as a special Christmas gift fer ya', Virgil. What if they end up bustin' it up and all? Then ya' don't have nuthin'. I don't right care if it was made by that damn Schilling, it's so very pretty. Is there no other way of provin' that chemist's theory?"

Deekie was distraught at the thought of losing forever the very first real gift she had ever given to her man that held both tangible and heartfelt meaning. She always wished to give him a keepsake. Something that was from her heart, not just a hand me down from somebody else.

"Ya' want yer Li'l Miss Essie to have a mother to care fer her?" Clay reminded her. "Ya' done said already to me that as much as ya' love that child, she belongs with her gypsy mama."

By then it was mid-morning and they were all in Sheriff Goff's office and jailhouse. Deekie looked over Clay's shoulder to glimpse Vadoma in her cell. She held her child Damara close to her heart. In that glimpse Deekie knew she could never replace the child's mama, causing her own heart to beat with an insufferable sadness. She knew this gypsy woman's future hinged on this test.

It must prove the professor's claim that the reason the German wanted to rework all those globes was to erase any evidence that he had used the toxic glycol fluid instead of the safer glycerin compound. To everyone's knowledge, the only specimen left thought to have that poison in it was Deekie's globe.

"Dang it, Virgil," she said to Clay, "don't lay this all on my hide. I done gave that snow globe to ya' Christmas morn, it's yer decision to make."

"No, I won't," Clay said adamantly. "I'll never hear the end of it fer as long as we live. No, this globe means too much to ya', so ya' gotta be the one to give the go-ahead. Only ya' can give *this thing* up."

It was perhaps how he pronounced those two words, *"this thing."* In them, she heard the echo of Hanzi's voice as he relayed the gypsy mother Vadoma's own advice, *"Do not play in the shadows of death, rid yourself of this thing."*

"Alright, Virgil," Deekie conceded, "let them go ahead and destroy it if it can prove she's innocent. I jus' wish we could somehow have it back afterward."

Clay took the globe from her, and began to pass it on to Dr. Lavoisier who was anxious to get down to Stegall's Station. Just as he moved his hand toward the professor, Deekie snatched the globe back from him and shook it hard.

"I jus' gotta see one more beautiful snowfall," she apologized, "it's so dang pretty." As she watched the white flakes clock and wheel like a flock of birds over the alpine village one last time, she wiped tears from her eyes and then handed the globe directly to Dr. Lavoisier.

It was late that afternoon, near dusk, that both sheriffs Goff and Pierce returned to the office from taking the other professor, Dr. Stevens, to Miss Margaret's home.

"Well, Deekie," Sheriff Goff said, "Dr. Stevens here may have solved another piece of this mystery for us."

"How so?" she asked.

"Recall that Miss Margaret complained to me that Herr Schilling was somehow killing her Christmas Roses?"

"Sure," Deekie said, "but both yerself and I went through that hot house, and not a one of them roses was less than perfect."

"That's because they're roses," Dr. Stevens, said, "and not Christmas Roses."

"Yer tryin' real hard to confuse me," Deekie said, "but what yer sayin' ain't nuthin' but gibberish to me."

"Here, let me try," said Goff. "Can ya' 'member tellin me about them shriveled up plants along the fence? Well, those plants aren't roses at all, at least not real roses."

"Helleborus niger," said the professor, likely knowing the sheriff would not remember the name of the plant. "They are commonly called Snow Roses, or Winter Roses. Or most often, Christmas Roses."

"So why would Miss Margaret git so riled up over those plants if they weren't real roses a't'all?" Clay asked.

"These Christmas Rose plants can be very difficult to grow, especially in this area," Dr. Stevens said. "They need sun in the winter, shade in the summer. Miss Margaret had them expertly located by that fence to take care of all that. Likely that runoff from the workshop was contaminating them, so they withered, which most likely angered our deceased master gardener to no end."

"Explain to me," Deekie called out, as if to signal she did not buy this explanation, "how a doctor of foreign tongues knows so much about plants and such?"

Doctor Stevens removed his coat and hung it on a peg on the wall. "Because I loved my mother, Miss Deekie. She was a biologist who specialized in plants. In fact, she loved roses, and taught me all about the *Helleborus niger,* so incredibly beautiful people called them Christmas Roses, even though they weren't roses at all. Then she taught me about its cousin, *Helleborus x hybridus,* which is called the Lenten Rose because it blooms purple at both Christmas and Easter time in the early spring. She said the *"x"* stood for the cross Our Lord had been crucified on. Perhaps I'm not much of a religious man these days, but I always remember how much my mother was."

"Such a touchin' tale," Deekie said, "but what's that got to do with studyin' all them foreign languages?"

"It's pretty simple really. Mama got me interested as a young boy as to why things are called what they are, and that led me to a life study of languages, starting with Latin, like the names of those flowers. A bit of our past often comes back to benefit us when we least expect it."

It was then when Dr. Lavoisier returned from Stegall's Station. His face was stern, and everyone feared the test had been a failure.

"Well, Dr. Lavoisier," asked Dr. Stevens, "was your hypothesis correct?"

"First, I have something to present to Miss Deekie," the professor said. He held out his hand and produced the snow globe, intact and unharmed in any way to her eyes. "Go ahead, take it and shake it." His eyes were alight with magic as he said these words, and a great smile creased his face, as if presenting a lost toy to a pouting child.

Deekie was overjoyed and grabbed the globe from his hand. She gave it a quick shake and the snow bloomed up in a squall, but as she watched, it settled out in a much quicker and more natural way. "It's beautiful. So ya' wasn't able to test it?"

"Oh, we most certainly tested it," Dr. Lavoisier answered. "And yes, Dr. Stevens, it confirmed my every suspicion. It was full of glycol, which as I have said can be as poisonous as Strychnine."

"Was?" Deekie looked incredulously at the globe in her hands. "Ya' mean it t'ain't no more? Not a't'all? How can that be?"

"Don't worry, Miss Deekie," the chemist said. "I was able to drain out all the pure glycol through a small hole drilled through its base on the underside. I replaced it with a very much diluted solution of glycerine in water and replugged the base. That will be entirely safe for you and your family. As you already noted, the diluted version looks better, and still won't freeze in even the worst winter you're ever likely to have around here."

"So what does all this mean in solving Miss Margaret's murder?" Clay asked.

"It means tonight I'll petition Judge Ferris at his home to release this young woman," Goff pointed in the direction of Vadoma, "so she can be released to return home with Sheriff Pierce and his other gypsy. It's pretty clear we now have enough to hold Herr Heinrich Schilling for the murder of old Miss Margaret. Well, maybe jus' manslaughter, as it doesn't appear the German thought to do it in advance. We may never know fer sure whatever sparked their quarrelin' that night in the first place, but it sure seems either his blow to her head with that snow globe or that poison leakin' outta it after it cracked open was what done killed her."

"And the dog too," Clay added.

"Thank God for that dead stray," Goff said, "and for Clay here noticing them flakes on its tongue. Without all that, and Miss Deekie's snow globe as the clincher, Schilling would likely have gotten away with all this by blaming it on the gypsy woman who couldn't defend herself."

It was then that Sheriff Goff noticed the two doctors from Franklin College exchanging odd looks.

"And of course," Goff was quick to add, "these two learned marvels came to town jus' in time to lend their unique skills and add the stamp of authority to these findings. Thank ya' both, good doctors."

"It is our honor," said Dr. Stevens, "to apply our knowledge and expertise to help liberate this poor woman."

"Best of all," Sheriff Pierce added, "this poor woman's soul will not be forever ruined."

Those words reminded Deekie one more time of that tender passage Miss Margaret had underlined from the Hunchback book. Those words kept coming back to her. She looked at Vadoma who still rested in her cell with the child drawn close to her heart. Deekie did not recite the author Victor Hugo's words, but instead reveled in the feel of them swirling within the interior of her own heart:

"Love is like a tree: it grows by itself, roots itself deeply in our being and continues to flourish over a heart in ruin." [24]

---

[24] Victor Hugo, "The Hunchback of Notre Dame," American Edition 1833.

Chapter Twenty-eight

The next morning, Deekie had just enough time to take Damara, as she now called the child, around to see Doc Hardin before going up to Sheriff Goff's office where she would meet up with her Virgil. The child had been through so much, and was not as docile as she had been earlier. She was fussing all the time, causing Deekie great concern. After examining her, Doc Hardin said she was cutting teeth and it appeared no more serious than that. This relieved Deekie to no end.

She and Damara arrived at the sheriff's office in time to celebrate. Judge Ferris had been briefed the night before, and after sleeping on it, agreed to allow the gypsy mother to be released. Sheriff Pierce took the three gypsies, Hanzi, Vadoma and her daughter, Damara, aboard the southbound train to Big Shanty. The two professors had earlier caught a train southbound to Atlanta, where they intended to spend a few days visiting the sights. Sheriff Goff and his Deputy Howard Gilmore were now transporting the prisoner Schilling back into the Sheriff's jail cells where he would be held until his hearing. The combination of all these activities now left Clay and Deekie alone in the depot as the train lurched away into the distance.

"Well, I'm right proud of ya', Deeks," Clay said.

"What fer, Virgil?"

"I'd reckoned ya'd be cryin' and blubberin' all over the place havin' to give yer Li'l Miss Essie back to her mama today," he went on. "I thought on yer sayin',

that life without a warming love is but a dry wheel, creaking and grating as it turns." [25]

"Those are that author's words, not my own," she confessed. "Besides, Virgil, yer the warmin' love of my life."

Then he said to her, "Deekie, I thought ya' would be all torn up over Li'l Miss Essie leavin' town with her mama. I know ya' was attached to her somethin' fierce."

"I was fer a spell," Deekie admitted, "until I saw the love between Damara - after all that's her name - and her mama. There is nothin' stronger or more beautiful than that love."

Clay thought, *Women, I don't reckon a man's been born yet that has figured them out.*

Then Deekie said, "Well, ya' best walk me over to the general store to git me a proper dress. Sheriff Goff was kind enough to leave me somethin' of a bonus on his desk that should cover the cost."

"A proper dress? Fer yerself?" Clay asked in a surprised tone. "Since when ya' been wantin to appear to be proper, Deeks?"

"Well, what else would y'expect me to wear to a weddin', Virgil?" she answered his question with her own.

---

[25] Victor Hugo, "The Hunchback of Notre Dame," American Edition 1833.

"What weddin? Who's gittin' hitched?"

"We are, that's who," she said flatly, leaving no room whatsoever for negotiation.

"What?" Clay said. "Why does that come as such a surprise to me?"

"That's right, Virgil. Ya' best be makin' an honest woman outta me iffen I'm gonna be carryin' yer chil' all over town," Deekie said as she patted her still flat belly. "Won't be long before I look like I done swallered a watermelon whole."

"Well, I'll be," said Clay as a proud and joyful grin flashed across his face. "How can this be?"

"Oh, it be!" she said. "Doc Hardin thinks so at least. After he tended to Miss Essie, when I told him how sickly I been feelin' the mornings, he gave me a once over and confirmed it. We're havin' a baby, Virgil - you and me. I swear that gypsy woman Vadoma done had somethin' to do with it."

"More than likely it is that I had somethin' to do with it," Clay smirked.

"Oh, ya' had somethin' to do with it all right," she replied, "and I can't wait to see our baby's face. Boy or girl don't matter, long as it has yer eyes, Virgil."

"A sharpshooter's eyes?" he playfully said

"No, an honest and good man's eyes."

She was serious and in no mood to play. She was being rewarded for the love and care she had shone to others. And it felt absolutely wonderful.

"I can't explain it," Deekie as she gave his lone arm a strong tug, placing his hand on her stomach, "but I know fer sure that this is real. Yer gonna be a *Diddy.*"

She thought of the months of waiting ahead, ever so lovingly, for their little angel to come forth, as another passage from the Hunchback novel rang out like the bells of Notre Dame Cathedral's within her head:

'Oh! love!' said she, and her voice trembled,
and her eye beamed. 'That is to be two and to be but
one. A man and a woman mingled into one angel.
It is heaven." [26]

---

[26] Victor Hugo, "The Hunchback of Notre Dame," American Edition 1833.

The trial of Herr Heinrich Schilling commenced in early February. The gypsies were long gone, their tribe had moved on from Sheriff Otho Pierce's Big Shanty jurisdiction to whereabouts unknown.

Yet this was exactly as the lawyers that were hired by the German had wanted. First they had the testimony of the gypsy woman, Vadoma, thrown out on the basis of it having been recorded by Truitt Clay-Harris, Clerk of the Court, but who also was also present at the murder scene that night. The lawyers argued that this allowed his recollections and biases to taint the transcription. Judge Ferris, ever a stickler for the conventions of jurisprudence, was forced to disallow its usage.

Once that was accomplished, it did not take much to seed the jury with the doubts that the death of the beloved townswoman, Miss Margaret Taylor-Smith, was the work of none other than the same gypsy woman that she had in her kindness taken in. The argument struck a chord in some of the jurors, as the defense presented Her Schilling as an industrious and well intentioned businessman who made beautiful *objects d'art.* It didn't help that the prosecution stumbled many times when presenting the chemistry of Dr. Laurent Lavoisier, who unfortunately could not be a witness at the trial as he was on sabbatical travels overseas.

Interestingly, Dr. Lavoisier would visit his relative, the famous chemist Antoine Lavoisier in Paris on that trip. Fate would find his visit fortunate, for in just less than two decades his French relative would be beheaded in the waning days of the Reign of Terror of the French Revolution in May of 1894. His famous relative, commonly known as *"the Father of Modern Chemistry"* was guillotined for the unforgivable sin of being a member of the class of aristocratic farm holders.

Relative to Herr Schilling's trial, the prosecution failed to gain a conviction. Nor was there an acquittal, but rather the result was a hung jury. "The Hun" was released, and no retrial was sought. Naturally, there was much talk after the fact was revealed that the jury was hung by the adamant and unflinching will of a single gentleman's vote. It was alleged but never proven that Herr Schilling had bought the man's favor.

The following month, Deekie and Clay had married in a very private ceremony on their homespread. Several months later, she gave birth to their first child. Clay held the infant in his arm, and secured it against the stump of his left arm, when it began to itch wildly. He looked up to the heavens and thought, *Thank ya', Colonel. I promised ya' I'd do some good on yer behalf.*

THE END OF

"Petals of the Christmas Rose"

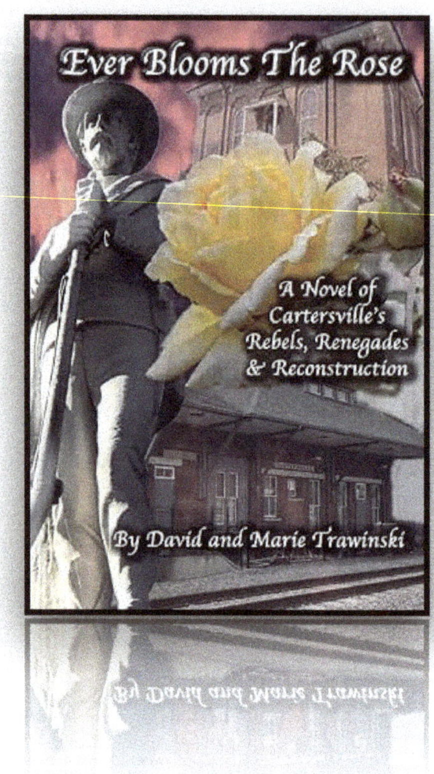

"Petals of the Christmas Rose," is the third Clay and Deekie novel by DAMTE Associates Publishing,

after "Ever Blooms the Rose" (2019) and

"Guns of the Yellow Rose" (2022).

Authors' Notes

We completed the initial draft of this novel later than we hoped, in the weeks just before Christmas 2024. Yet that proved inspiring for a couple reasons. First, we were immersed in the Christmas spirit and hopefully some of that seeped into this work. Secondly, just as we finished, the Cathedral of Notre Dame in Paris reopened after the horrendous fire of 2019. Not only was it restored, but gleamed and glistened brighter than what we had seen in person on a number of visits. How interesting that this reopening converged with our use of Hugo's classic in this story!

We love writing the Clay and Deekie characters. Clay is such a humble but tortured soul, left less than whole by the war but somehow in many ways is more complete a man than those who never fought. Deekie, on the other hand, is more of a free spirit, curious and easily distracted, but always does what needs to be done by each story's end. She loves the distraction of reading, and is always aching to get her hands on books as there were no community libraries yet at that time.

We are blessed to have such a rich choice of research materials at our fingertips. First there are the local gems: The Bartow County History Museum and its archives; the Etowah Valley Historical Society, and even in some of our novels the Booth Western Art Museum. Cartersville is certainly blessed in these treasures, and in those who have made and continue to make them possible. Finally, we now have access to the on-line versions of documents like never before.

We always had the idea for this story to feature a peddler of roses on the town's streets, with the play on words with the title - "pedal" vs. "petal." That led us to make our rose peddler a gypsy, and after research we learned that indeed there were *Romani* people in America, and more specifically in north Georgia in 1875.

Perhaps the readers have noticed Deekie's love of reading as an escape. In our first offering, *"Ever Blooms the Rose"* she consumed the collected stories of Edgar Allen Poe. In the western adventure *"Guns of the Yellow Rose,"* her Virgil bought her Melville's *"Moby Dick."* So it was only natural that in this volume, Deekie would work her way through Victor Hugo's classic *"Notre Dame de Paris,"* or as it was known in America, *"The Hunchback of Notre Dame."*

A little about our German antagonist, *Herr Heinrich Schilling.* He is completely fictional, but why German? For two reasons. First, snow globes were created in this timeframe (within a few years of 1875, in any case) in Vienna, Austria.

Second, the discovery of the class of chemicals known as glycols were developed just before this time in Strasbourg in the Alsace region that historically has passed back and forth between France and Germany. (David apologizes if his explanations of the chemistry in this novel is not clear enough - it's been only about forty years or so since he got his undergraduate degree in Chemistry.) In the end, to make the story work, we needed a German glassblower who would have had access to both of these historical events.

The professors from Franklin College, the original name of the University of Georgia, are fictional. However, Professor Lavoisier is named after the very real Antoine-Laurent de Lavoisier, the father of modern chemistry who so tragically was beheaded late in the French Revolution. He was exonerated only a year and a half later, and it was said of his death, *"It took them only an instant to cut off this head, and one hundred years might not suffice to reproduce its like."*

Why the homage to Colonel Lewis Tumlin? Well, we attended the Oak Hill Cemetery Candlelight Ghost Tour one Halloween and were very impressed by the guides' reverence for this father of Cartersville. What a wonderful night that proved to be, and what a wonderful man this was. So we found our own way to keep his memory alive - it seemed only fitting he should open and close our little story. We fictionalized the Colonel very minimally, only in his kindness toward Clay and Deekie. We hope that is viewed to be most respectful.

Our fictional treatment of Mr. John T. Owen and the unnamed druggist at Sayre's Pharmacy we also hope is viewed as nothing less than respectful. Both characters were drawn from nothing more than the advertisement in the Cartersville Express. We could not find the exact placement of Sayre's on Main Street, but research by Joe Head of the Etowah Valley Historical Society suggests it was on the block between the Western and Atlantic Railroad tracks and Erwin Street. His research also shows that Asa Griggs Candler (the man who would later purchase the Coca Cola formula from Mr. John S. Pemberton and go on to found the world famous brand) once worked at it's predecessor, Kilpatrick and Sayre Pharmacy here in Cartersville. While the precise storefront location of Sayre's remains a mystery, Mr. Head's research shows it is almost certainly was not at the corner Young's Pharmacy held (where later the first Coca Cola sign would be so boldly painted to catch the attention of railcar passengers) as that building did not exist at that location in 1875.

Just like Clay, Deekie and Truitt, Sheriff Alpheus T. Goff, Judge Ferris and Doc Hardin are fully fictional characters. Well, in reality the name Alpheus T. Goff is borrowed from Marie's ancestor who indeed fought in the Civil War. Judge Ferris and Doc Hardin are sheer creations of our imagination, and as they say any similarities to persons living or deceased are mere coincidences.

As we said, we love writing these *"Rose"* stories and have a few more in mind to continue on with. We have been overwhelmed with the response we have gotten to them, both from readers around town and others across the country who might likely think Cartersville itself is a fictional place. To our benefit, it is very real indeed, and we feel ourselves most lucky to be included among its citizens.

David and Marie Trawinski

Appendix A: Source Materials and Suggested Readings

1: "The Light of Other Days," Caroline Couper Lovell (1862 - 1947), Mercer University Press, 1995, Macon, Georgia.

> *Originally written in the 1930s, the author recalls her childhood in Cartersville and Bartow County. She was thirteen years old and escaping the summer heat of her Savannah Georgia home by visiting her family in Bartow County at the time of this story in 1875.*

2. "Sketches of Bartow County," by J. B. Tate et al., Etowah Valley Historical Society, Cartersville, Georgia.

> *Wonderful non-fiction historical treatises of Bartow County by several local historians and authors.*

3. History of Bartow County, Georgia (Formerly Cass), by Lucy Josephine Cunyus, 1932.

> *An extremely well documented accounting of the history of the county during the author's lifetime.*

4. "The Hunchback of Notre Dame (Notre Dame de Paris)" by Victor Hugo, American Edition, 1833.

> *A true classic of love, faith, devotion and forgiveness in fifteenth century Paris. Quotes used throughout this version are public domain.*

And, Of Course, We Are Very Much Indebted to:

> *The Bartow County History Museum and its Archives,*
>
> *The Etowah Valley Historical Society*
>
> *Digital Library of Georgia's, Galileo's and UGA Library's Georgia Historic Newspapers On-Line Site Funded by the RJ Taylor Foundation.*

Appendix B: List of Cover and Interior Image Credits
(Image numbers referred to licensed Adobe Stock Images)

Front Cover Layout Design by David Trawinski
utilizing the following licensed Adobe Stock Images
Christmas village and tree inside a snow globe,
 # 548884179 by Vuang
Cracked Glass # 617269160 by malshak_off
Rose Blossom #565530758 by Natural PNG

Copyright page - Rose Petals #742551292 by RM Graphics
Rose Image #245036112 by Ekaterina

Chapter Headings and Dividers and used throughout -
Rose Image # 245036112

"Map of Cartersville 1875"
Created by David Trawinski © 2025 utilizing:
Rose Image # 245036112 by Ekaterina, and
"Natural Cream Marble Texture Background"
Image #306206996 by Vidal

Portrait of Victor Hugo made from: Hugo Portrait #661966833 by
Yacine and Notre Dame de Paris Portrait #962035564 by Yotwarit

Figure 1: US Trade Dollar 1875, Public Domain Image, Wikimedia
Figure 2: Borden's Eagle Brand Condensed Milk, Public Domain
Image, Wikimedia
Figure 3: Park and BraBan Hotel Images,
Public Domain Postcard Images

Page 217: Cover Images of "Ever Blooms the Rose" and
"Guns of the Yellow Rose"
© DAMTE Associates Publishing LLC with
"Realistic red roses border..." Adobe image # 318239586
by WinWin.

Back Cover Layout Design by David Trawinski
utilizing the following licensed Adobe Stock Images:
Notre Dame Snow Globe - David Trawinski via Firefly
Snowy Background - David Trawinski via Firefly
Rose Garland #318239536 by WinWin
Depot and Courthouse Overlays provided by the
Bartow County History Museum

"Petals of the Christmas Rose"
Is Proudly Published by

www.ingramcontent.com/pod-product-compliance
Lightning Source LLC
Chambersburg PA
CBHW041051310726
48978CB00011BA/511